"To first dates."

Tom raised his glass. "To the Japanese railway."

"To the end of fashionable lateness."

He leaned closer. "To Fate in all its infinite wisdom." He rose and stood so close that the heat from his body made Katie sway at its source. She took a small step backward.

"To getting dinner ready on time." She clicked her glass against his.

"To hell with dinner." He took her glass and put it down on the end table with his.

Katie's breath caught as he turned back to her and looked in her eyes. "I didn't come here only for the lasagna."

His hands were at her waist, the tips of his thumbs at the bottom of her rib cage. "I didn't think so."

You can stop this now if you want to, Katie told herself. *All you have to do is smile and turn away.*

But she did neither.

BARBARA BRETTON

SHOOTING STAR

MIRA BOOKS

ISBN 1-55166-074-1

SHOOTING STAR

Copyright © 1986 by Barbara Bretton.

Printed in U.S.A.

For Grandma Becker
For Uncle Barry Miller
For Louie Bagarozzi
Godspeed.

ACKNOWLEDGMENT

Many thanks to Rhonda Bagarozzi, whose
knowledge of and love for the people and country of Japan
helped me tremendously

and

To Danielle and Carlos Ortiz, our dearest friends, who took
this trip in the first place. Here's to changing zip codes in '86!
(So long, Speonk....)

1

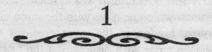

August 16 Japan

Tom Sagan could light up the night sky with tendrils of silver and gold; he could create white and amber chrysanthemums that burned brighter than the aurora borealis; he could lasso Saturn with glittering red rings that would shame the most beautiful star.

For three weeks he'd been traveling through Japan trying to make the secrets of the Flower-Scattering Child and the Gold Monkey and the Silver-Tailed Comet his own. He'd been to Tondabayashi for the Perfect Liberty Festival; he'd been to Miyazaki on the island of Kyushu, where the shells were shot across the width of the Oyodo River, trailing perfect plumes of royal purple and gold against the summer night sky.

Tomorrow morning he would travel to Kyoto to meet with Toshiro Umeki, an artist whose impressionist paintings had inspired some of the Ogatsu family's best fireworks.

Nowhere has he seen anyone able to turn copper salts and chlorine into a deep-blue flame as bright as it was beautiful. Blue was the last color added to the palette of pyrotechnics and the color most dangerous to create.

The only way Sagan Fireworks, Inc. was going to win the Second Biennial International Fireworks Competition in Las Vegas next month was to make the night sky over his hometown come alive with the same blue flame incongruously hidden in the most precious of emeralds—a feat on a par with discovering the Lost Ark.

Indiana Jones had succeeded.

So far Tom Sagan hadn't.

The Quieroz family in Brazil had come close, producing a slightly tarnished cobalt that had won them the contest in Monte Carlo last year. Now it was rumored that the great Ogatsu family, the Michelangelos of pyrotechnics, had created a blue that throbbed with intensity and clarity. That rumor had brought Tom thousands of miles from home to find out.

This trip up Mount Myojogatake for the sacred Daimonji Yaki, or bonfire ceremony, was his last chance to check out the competition. The Ogatsu family was staging the fireworks, and if any of his competitors had conquered the elusive blue flame, it would be the Ogatsus.

Tom was tired and lonely, eager for the pleasure of conversation after so much solitude. Having so much time to think had proved as much a burden as a blessing. This was to have been a time of renewal as well as research, a regrouping of his emotional forces—so badly battered—before he set out upon the task of winning the competition.

Winning could never fill the empty places in his heart, but it could at least provide a fitting memorial to those he had loved and lost. At the very least, they deserved that small measure of immortality. He'd failed his father and fiancée in every other way possible.

He was deep in thought, oblivious to the throng of passengers surrounding him on the platform of the Hakone Tozan Railway, when he felt a tug on his pants leg and looked down at a little Japanese boy who wore a New York Yankees cap pulled down over his ears. Tom's pensive mood vanished as quickly as it had come.

"Are you going to the festival, too?" Tom crouched down to the boy's eye level and laughed as the child touched Tom's curly blond hair.

The child's mother laughed nervously. *"Sumimasen."*

It sounded like an apology. Tom smiled and stood up. "Don't worry," he said in English. "I like children."

Their intentions were clear, but it was obvious that neither Tom nor the woman understood each other. With a great deal of awkward smiling and bowing, the young mother moved down the narrow platform with her little boy, who kept turning around to wave goodbye to Tom.

He wondered why he hadn't noticed the crowds before. The last time he'd seen a throng like this was when he'd gotten himself lost in the New York City subway system a few years back.

Now, the Hakone Tozan Railway was hardly the BMT—for one thing, the passengers were certainly more polite—but the feeling of being fenced in was there just the same.

He towered over everyone else on the platform, feeling isolated and very foreign. Where were all the American tourists he'd figured he'd bump into? Where were all the retired schoolteachers he'd hoped to share the ride with, schoolteachers who just happened to speak fluent Japanese?

He was a talker, and the most frustrating thing about traveling alone through a strange country was the inability to communicate his feelings through anything more complex than sign language.

A high, piercing whistle drew his attention to the small hill just beyond the station. The train, older and more dilapidated than he'd expected, rattled into view, then wheezed to a stop at the platform.

The crowd swarmed through the open doors. Tom was swept along, surprised at the narrow benches and lazily rotating ceiling fans inside. He ended up wedged against the far wall, his head awkwardly angled to keep his hair from being chopped into a punk crew cut by the fan's blades.

Two elderly women were seated on the bench directly in front of him. They nodded and smiled up at Tom, talking softly between them, their almond-shaped eyes twinkling.

He reddened and looked away, directing his gaze out the open window to where still more passengers waited to board. They'd better be waiting for the next train, because the one he was on didn't have room for the fleas on a toy poodle.

Suddenly he caught the glitter of sun-streaked copper and he shifted his position, straining for a better look. Long waves of auburn hair tumbled over the shoulders of a tall, slender woman in a blue-and-white-striped sundress. Her back was to him, but judging by the sweetly curved waist and hips, this was no retired schoolteacher spending her pension money on a world tour.

If she was a schoolteacher, he would have to think very seriously of repeating some of his more elementary education.

The crowd on the platform moved again, and just as the doors to his railroad car creaked closed, she disappeared from view.

If Lady Luck was on his side, she was in the next car.

It was a long ride up the mountain to the station at Gora. Passing the time of day with a fellow American would make the time go much faster.

He thought of the way her hair sparkled in the summer sun and grinned. He didn't even care if she could speak Japanese.

The rickety railroad car shuddered, lurched, then sputtered to a stop, and Katie Powers was sure she was about to die. She could see the headlines in the Tokyo papers now: "Foolish American Tourist Should Have Known Better Than to Listen to Sister."

"Oh, Gwen," Katie muttered, ignoring the curious glances of the little Japanese girl who shared the seat with her, "why did I listen to you?" The little girl, who until now had been fascinated by Katie's hair, scooted as far away as the narrow seat would allow.

Every seat on the train was filled and every inch of standing room taken as well. Compared with the swift, ultramodern Shinkansen, on which the Bullet train had taken her out of Tokyo, this tiny conveyance seemed a relic from the days of the samurai and the shoguns. Katie wasn't sure they would reach the Gora station before the end of the next millennium.

She lifted her thick, wavy hair off the back of her neck. The open window next to her provided little relief, for the air was still and hot, heavy with the summer scent of flowers.

The train groaned ominously. Katie glanced out the window, shuddering at the distance between herself and the ground below. Well, at least she wouldn't have to worry about being roasted alive anymore. Crashing into the ravine below would definitely cool her off.

Fine for Gwen to say "Be daring." It wasn't Gwen who was trapped on the train.

"The Daimonji Yaki only happens one night a year, Katie," Gwen had said that morning as she dressed for work. Gwen was a free-lance translator who'd been asked at the last minute to fill in at the American Embassy. "Just because I have to work doesn't mean you should miss out."

Katie had hesitated. "I don't know...."

Gwen made a face and tapped her sister on the head with her hairbrush. "I've seen it three times already. The spirits will find their way to earth just fine without me this year." The Obon, a six-day commemoration, when the beloved dead ancestors visited their earthly homes, began on August 15, and on the night of August 16 the Daimonji Yaki was lit—a ritual of flames and fireworks—in honor of the spirits.

"It won't be the same without you." Having a sister who spoke fluent Japanese had been like having a personal tour guide.

"Don't miss it on my account, Katie." Gwen thought for a moment. "How about I meet you for dinner at the hotel near the Chokoku no Mori station afterward? Say, about ten?"

"You're beginning to sway me," Katie said.

"We'll even spend the night," Gwen said. "You didn't come halfway around the world to hang around my apartment watching my plants grow, did you?"

"Do I have to dignify that with an answer?" Katie couldn't help laughing. Gwen had been haranguing Katie about her tendency to choose the well-traveled road since she had arrived in Tokyo at the beginning of the month.

The look Gwen gave Katie could only be described as that of Condescending Older Sister Number One. "You'll have plenty of time to settle into a rut when you go back to Boston," Gwen said. "Live dangerously for a few hours, Katie. Danger is good for the soul."

Well, it was hard to imagine anything more dangerous than her present predicament, unless it was tightrope walking across the Grand Canyon. And if Gwen had any ideas about that, Katie would be glad to send her sister a plane ticket for Arizona with her best wishes.

All Katie wanted was to get off this train alive.

A conductor pushed his way into the front of the railroad car and said something quick and low to two young women in the first row. The prettier of the two clutched the other's hand and Katie's heart plunged to the bottom of the ravine, where she was sure the rest of her body would soon follow.

"Wait a minute!"

The man turned at the sound of Katie's voice but looked at her blankly. Damn! What were the Japanese words for "Wait a minute"?

"*Chotto-matte,*" she said. The conductor smiled, obviously pleased at her attempt to speak his language. "*Wakarimasen.*" "I don't understand what's happening here."

The conductor explained their situation quite cheerfully, although twice Katie had to interrupt him with "*Yukkuri,*" a plea for him to speak more slowly.

Apparently the train was in no great danger, but a portion of track behind them had snapped, catching the undercarriage of the car Katie was riding in. A repair crew was patching it up now and the train would soon be limping its way up to Gora and Mount Myojo.

"*Domo arigato,*" she thanked him, self-consciously rolling her "r" as Gwen had instructed.

Katie sat back down on her seat, feeling slightly less certain she was about to meet her Maker. The little girl next to her scurried back to sit with her mother, as if she'd decided this redheaded American with the terrible Japanese accent was most untrustworthy. Katie obviously wasn't making any friends, but at least she had gained a bit more elbow room. On the crowded train, that was not something to be taken lightly.

She'd been aware of her foreignness while touring Tokyo and the environs with Gwen; it was impossible for a tall redhead to blend in with the rest of the population. She'd rather enjoyed being the center of so much benevolent attention. But here, away from the tourist meccas and without Gwen's expertise, she felt awkward and out of place. The sight of a huge electronic bulletin board of train information—all in Japanese— at the railroad station in Tokyo had sent her spiraling into a minor panic, as her limitations were sharply defined.

Gaijin, the word for outsider, took on meanings her schoolgirl's grasp of the language hadn't prepared her for.

A blast of hot air, mingled with the smell of exhaust, had just set Katie thinking about how she'd sell her passport for an interpreter and an ice-cold Pepsi when someone squeezed into the narrow seat next to her.

"I knew I heard an American voice," a male voice said. "I was hoping it belonged to you."

A large hand popped up in front of Katie's face and she turned around in her seat. A man with a full head of dark blond hair smiled at her, his white teeth gleaming beneath a full mustache. He picked up her hand from her lap and shook it firmly.

"I'm Tom Sagan," he said, "intrepid traveler. I saw your red hair on the platform before we boarded but I lost sight of you in the push. When I heard you talking with the conductor, I had to track you down." He released her hand from his grip. "Now don't tell me I should have made out my will before I left home."

Katie was so relieved to hear English, she could have kissed him. She introduced herself instead.

"What's the matter?" he asked. "You look like you've just seen a ghost." His eyes widened. "Are we going to have to be airlifted out of here like extras in a Sylvester Stallone movie?"

Katie burst out laughing. That was only the second time the man had stopped for breath. "I think you'd enjoy it if we were. I hate to disappoint you, but it's only a delay." She explained about the piece of track embedded in the undercarriage of the train. "It'll just take us longer to get up to the Gora station, that's all."

He leaned back in his seat and wiped imaginary sweat from his brow. "What a relief." His eyes were beautiful, a deep, rich topaz framed by thick, curly eyelashes. Judging by the fine lines at the outer corners, Katie figured him to be in his early thirties. "I was afraid I would have to do my Spiderman act." He mimed ripping his white cotton shirt open and exposing a superhero's costume.

"Too bad you were cheated out of the chance." Actually, it was too bad *she* had been cheated out of seeing what appeared to be a decidedly superhero body. The thin shirt covered a lean, well-muscled torso that was tanned the same golden color as his eyes.

The rows of benches afforded little leg room, and Tom Sagan's long body was wedged into the seat. He moved around in a futile attempt to get comfortable and his right shoulder bumped companionably into hers. "Sorry." He rubbed her left shoulder with strong, sure fingers. "They don't make these seats for American builds."

"Or the showers. Every time I wash my hair, I have to kneel down in order to use the spray."

Tom's laugh filled the small railway car. "I have the same problem."

She could easily imagine his tall, muscular body twisting into contortions in a tiny shower stall.

"So, Katie Powers, what brings you to Japan? Business or pleasure?"

"I'm between jobs and I thought I'd visit my sister while I considered my options."

"Very sensible," Tom said. "But I'm disappointed."

Katie arched one auburn brow. "Why would you be disappointed?"

"Too mundane and practical. When I saw you standing on the platform at Odawara, I came up with this whole exotic past for you, complete with covert operations and secret identities." He shook his shaggy blond head. "And you tell me you're here to see your sister. Very unimaginative, Katie Powers. Very unimaginative.''

Now that he mentioned it, it did sound rather unimaginative at that. "You'd rather I told you I'm an undercover spy sent here by a hostile government to figure out the secrets of the Daimonji fireworks?''

"If you tell me that, then you've met your match, because that's exactly why I'm here.''

"You're a fireworks spy?'' His imagination was something to ponder.

He looked as if he were trying the idea on for size. "I guess you could call me a fireworks spy. I'm checking out the festival displays for my family's company.''

"Oh, sure.'' She was unable to keep the chuckle from her voice. "And you've been going from Osaka to Kyoto to Hakone to check them all, right?''

"Exactly.'' He grinned, his golden eyes catching the light. "Except you forgot Monte Carlo.''

"Monte Carlo!'' Katie slapped the heel of her hand to her forehead and groaned. "How on earth could I forget Monte Carlo? Any good spy would go to Monte Carlo to check out the fireworks.''

"Now that I've blown my cover, what's your mission on Mount Myojo?''

She had already told him that she was between jobs and considering her options. She could also tell him she was visiting her sister and brother-in-law; she could tell him she'd hoped getting away from Boston would blast her out of the depression she'd been in since her ex-husband became a first-time father with his new wife. All true statements.

All incredibly dull.

She was thousands of miles away from her old life, her old memories. If this Tom Sagan was going to be so outrageous, why shouldn't she?

She glanced around furtively. "It's top secret."

Tom leaned closer. "I've been cleared by Security. You can trust me."

"I'm carrying the secret formula for the old Coca-Cola somewhere on my person." She rearranged her bangle bracelet over her wrist.

Tom looked at her wrist. "Tattoo?"

"Special ink. It's only visible on the night of August sixteenth."

"The stars have to be in a special position?"

"And there have to be fireworks. Lots of them."

"Who's your connection in Hakone?" he asked. "Could it possibly be—"

"Oh, no. You'll never get that out of me, Sagan."

"Shh." He put his finger to his lips. "The code name is Smith."

"I'll keep that in mind."

The train was hot, cramped and wretchedly uncomfortable, and Katie hoped they'd be stuck for hours. She hadn't felt this wonderful in a long, long time.

Tom Sagan rarely found himself at a loss for words, but when Katie Powers flashed him a full-powered smile, his brain turned to chalk dust. He was still trying to come up with something clever to say when the train rumbled to life again beneath him. Damn it to hell. He felt like slipping the engineer a few thousand yen to make this trip last a little longer.

Two or three lifetimes would do.

The last time he'd felt like this was when he'd sent up three perfect split comets whose golden tendrils had laced the night sky.

A conductor stopped by Tom and Katie and said something in a combination of Japanese and indecipherable English.

"Why aren't you smiling?" Tom asked as the conductor moved on to the next row of seats. "Are we going to have to walk the rest of the way?"

Katie looked out the window and down at the earth far below. "Not without a parachute." The train inched forward once more. "Everything's under control. He promises we'll be there by six o'clock."

Was he crazy, or did she look as disappointed as he felt?

"Where did you learn to speak Japanese? I'm impressed."

"Part of my training," she said. "The company expects its operatives to fit into their surroundings."

He surprised himself when he reached over and tugged at a lock of her wavy auburn hair. It slid through his fingers like satin. "Sorry, Katie, but you'll never fit into these surroundings with this."

She gestured toward his own curly blond hair. "That's not exactly government issue you have there, Sagan."

He'd forgotten their spy scenario. His brain clicked back into gear. "It's all part of my disguise. I'm actually a double agent, trained to baffle even the most beautiful of the villains that the enemy sends my way."

"Poor thing," she said. "You must have your hands full."

His sigh was loud, long and very theatrical. "It's a nasty business. Blondes, brunettes..." He paused for a second, then grinned. "Even an occasional redhead."

"Watch out for the redheads. They can be deadly."

"Which is it then: poison perfume or a hidden derringer?"

"Trade secret."

"You're a tough customer, Powers. I'm glad we're on the same side."

"So am I."

Again that killer smile of hers. He felt it all the way down to his toes.

Suddenly he wanted to know everything about her. "So, what brings you here, Katie?"

She looked over at him and shrugged her tanned shoulders. "Same as you, I would imagine. The Daimonji Festival."

"You came all the way from the States for it? It's not exactly a well-known celebration off the islands."

"My sister, Gwen, lives in Tokyo," Katie said, apparently dropping her secret-agent pose. "She's married to a Japanese doctor and she's become totally immersed in Japanese culture. It was her idea to travel up to Mount Myojo for the fireworks, but an assignment came up and—" she shrugged "—here I am, one lone American adrift in the Land of the Rising Sun." She lifted her hair off the back of her neck and he thought he'd never seen such a graceful, erotic gesture. "What brings you here?"

"Fireworks."

"Seriously, Tom."

"Fireworks." He grinned at the look of suspicion on her lovely face. "I told you before."

"We were kidding before."

"Maybe you were, but I wasn't. My family owns a fireworks company in Las Vegas."

She stared at him.

"What's the matter?" he asked, laughing. "Did I sprout a slot machine under my arm?"

Katie still looked doubtful. "I suppose you're here to check out the competition?"

"Now you've got the idea. The Japanese create works of art with their pyrotechnics, and I'm not above trying to figure out what the hell their secret is before the next contest."

"What will you do with their secret when you figure it out? Steal it?"

"Harsh words, Katie. Let's just say I'll borrow it."

He detected a twinkle in her lovely blue eyes. "You must admit the premise seems a bit absurd."

"Guilty."

"I mean, that's a lot of trouble to go to for something that's pertinent just once a year, isn't it?"

"You haven't done your homework, Agent Powers. Fireworks displays can be found anytime, anyplace."

"Granted, if you travel around the world hunting them up, but what about—"

"I'm not speaking internationally. I mean right in the good old U.S. of A."

"The only time I see fireworks is the Fourth of July."

How many times had he heard that? "If we relied on Independence Day celebrations to carry us, the business would've gone under twenty years ago. We do a hell of a lot more."

"This isn't a joke? You really do own a fireworks business?"

"Katie, Katie, why don't you believe what I say the first time? Sagan Fireworks has been around since right after World War Two. We're an institution."

"I'm impressed."

He grinned. "I was hoping you would be."

"So if you don't spend your time waiting for the Fourth to roll around each year, what *do* you do?"

Obviously the men in her life lived more normal lives. He decided to give her his best chamber of commerce spiel. "Being based in Vegas gives us lots of business opportunities. We do displays for trade shows and conventions, promo work for the hotels in town, not to mention the out-of-state jobs." He pushed his thick hair off his forehead with the back of his hand. "Venetian Night in Chicago, Shea Stadium in New York, Reagan's inauguration. We even orchestrate small shows for weddings and sweet sixteens."

"Orchestrate? What's so hard about setting off a few rockets and sparklers?"

"We choreograph the effects to music now. It's become a whole multimedia project."

Katie shook her head. "It's so far beyond my frame of reference that I can't even come up with any intelligent questions. I guess I've always believed fireworks simply happened."

"Spontaneous combustion?"

"Something like that. The end result is so magnificent, I've never even thought about how it all came about."

"You're not supposed to," Tom said. "It's like going to a puppet show: When you see the strings being pulled, the illusion is destroyed. We like to keep our strings invisible."

"You said something about a contest?"

The woman's curiosity was remarkable. "In September, every two years. I guess you could call it the World Series of Fireworks."

She started laughing.

"I'm insulted," he said, although he really wasn't. "You wouldn't laugh if I said I played for the Yankees."

"I probably would. I'm a Red Sox fan."

So she was from Boston? That would explain some of that Yankee caution she seemed to have. "We don't have pro baseball in Vegas," he said. "We have fireworks festivals."

"And you're the Mickey Mantle of the fireworks set?"

"I'll tell you the second week of September." His smile was easy; it just managed to hide the intense need that had brought him to Japan. He didn't want to think about that right now; he wanted to concentrate on the way Katie was making him feel.

The conductor came back into their car and made another announcement. Japanese spoken slowly was a difficult enough language; Japanese spoken at the rate of machine-gun fire was an impossible language. Tom looked to Katie for a translation.

"Let's see...something about the track behind us...damn, he's talking so fast...okay, now I've got it." She looked at Tom. "We'll be pulling into the station in five minutes."

"All that for such a short message?"

"Let's just say that's the *Reader's Digest* condensed version." She fanned herself with the magazine on her lap. The scent of Shalimar, faint and lovely, drifted over to him.

"What are your plans?" he asked, looking at his watch. "There's still two and a half hours until the ceremony."

She reached into her pocketbook and withdrew a handwritten map. "There's a tiny restaurant just beyond the Open Air Museum, and I intend to drink every can of Pepsi they have on hand."

He laughed. "I like a woman with a purpose in life."

The train slowly pulled into the station; its brakes sounded like the death cry of a prehistoric animal as it came to a bone-jarring halt. The doors creaked open. Tom made no move to leave, effectively trapping Katie in her seat. This was no time for subtlety.

"So what happens after you drink all that Pepsi?"

She looked up at the crowd filing past, then back at him. "Foolish question. I search for the nearest Western-style bathroom in Hakone."

"Practical as well as beautiful." He was stalling for time. They were the only people left on the train.

"And what are your plans?" she asked, a small smile curving her lips.

He hadn't known until that moment. Now it seemed as clear as the impossible blue of her eyes. "I'm going to spend the night with you."

2

Katie stared at him. "It must be the altitude. I can't believe you said that."

"I did." His smile was wide and innocent.

So much for friendly conversation. Tom Sagan apparently had dialogue of another kind in mind. "It's been an interesting ride. Enjoy your fireworks." She pushed past him.

"Katie! Wait!"

She ignored him and got off the train, letting herself get swept up in the crowd. Unfortunately, there was no way on earth she could blend in with the masses. In an instant he was next to her.

"You have quite a temper." He fell into step with her. "I'll have to keep that in mind."

"Press that thought in your memory book, because this is the last stop."

"A beautiful woman who's practical and has a sense of humor." She could hear suppressed laughter in his voice and she wanted to kick him in the kneecap. "Will you marry me?"

"Go to hell, Mr. Sagan. Go directly to hell. Do not pass Go. Do not collect two hundred dollars." A few fireworks must have gone off too close to his brain. He seemed to have difficulty understanding the brush-off when he heard it.

"Insults are lost on me. I have the hide of a rhinoceros."

"And the intellect of one. Read my lips: Leave me alone."

"How can I leave you alone when we have a job to do, Katie Powers? The agency needs us. Our country's depending on us."

"Sorry." She followed the crowd up a steep flight of stone stairs that would have left a marathoner gasping for breath. "I quit. You're on your own."

"America needs you."

Tom raced ahead of her. He didn't even have the good grace to appear winded by his exertions. Damn his long legs, anyway.

"You can't turn your back on your country."

"No, but I can turn my back on you." She had to turn her back on him. An idiotic smile was beginning to break across her face.

"You're abandoning me in a strange country?"

"I found you in a strange country, I can abandon you in a strange country."

"You're heartless." Tom moved back into her line of vision. "I wouldn't have expected that of you."

"Lower your voice. You're attracting a crowd."

Hakone was not a tourist mecca; the sight of an American was unusual enough. The sight of a tall, blond American man flirting shamelessly with a red-haired American woman was irresistible. They were ringed by smiling people.

"She's abandoning me," he said to the crowd at large. "Leaving me to fend for myself."

"They don't understand you, Sagan." Katie's face was as red as her hair.

"You'd leave me alone and I can't even speak the language?"

"What would you have done if we hadn't met?"

"But we did meet. We're in Fate's hands."

"I'm from Boston," she said. "We don't believe in Fate."

"I'm from Vegas and we light candles to it. Lady Luck is our patron saint."

The crowd settled down as if for a matinee performance. Katie, who usually avoided center stage, found herself caught up in the sheer silliness of the whole situation.

She continued up the hill toward the Open Air Museum in Chokoku no Mori. The crowd—and Tom—came with her.

"You might as well give up, Katie Powers. You're stuck with me."

She ignored him.

He pointed toward a road sign written in *kanji* characters.

"I'm helpless," he said. "I can't tell a rest room from a restaurant. I'll end up embarrassing myself in a sushi bar."

"If you need an interpreter, I'll give you my sister Gwen's number. Helpless cases are her specialty."

"Is she as beautiful as you are?" Katie stumbled, and Tom cupped her elbow to steady her. "I'm partial to redheads."

"Gwen's a blonde."

"I have nothing against blondes."

"Gwen's a married blonde."

"That could be a problem."

"If you knew Hiro, you'd know exactly how big a problem. You'd better light another candle because you're out of luck, Sagan. *Sayonara.*"

"*Sayonara* yourself." He matched his stride to hers.

"*Sayonara* means goodbye."

"I'm not totally ignorant," Tom said as they entered the Open Air Museum. "I saw the movie. Marlon Brando and—"

"You're not going to give up, are you?"

He shook his head, his thick curls sparkling like gold in the setting sun. "That's not how we won the West."

She glanced around at the Japanese faces surrounding them and at the white flag with the Rising Sun fluttering overhead. "This isn't the West."

"The principle's still the same. Tenacity's my middle name."

"I can think of a few that suit you better." She couldn't keep the chuckle from her voice.

"No profanity, please. You'll shatter my illusions about you."

"You've already told me I'm heartless. How many illusions could be left?"

"I'll tell you on our first anniversary. You'll be surprised."

"Somehow I don't think I'd be surprised by anything about you, Tom Sagan."

"Dangerous words," he said, glancing at his watch. "You've only known me three hours and forty-five minutes. I hope I still have a few surprises hidden up my sleeve."

She looked at his tanned, well-developed forearms. "You don't even have *sleeves* up your sleeves. I think I'm safe."

"I'm insulted."

"You shouldn't be. When I insult you, you'll know it."

"I've done my best to convince you I'm a dangerous spy," he said. "Safety isn't what you've been aiming at."

"I know exactly what you've been aiming at. That's what started this whole thing."

He stopped smack in front of an enormous sculpture labeled "Ms. Black Power." The love beads someone had placed around the statue's neck tinkled in the evening breeze.

"Maybe it *is* the altitude," he said, "because I don't understand a damned thing that's been going on since we got off the train."

"You must admit you were pretty outrageous."

He was watching her carefully, those golden eyes of his genuinely confused. "Listen, I thought you realized all that spy talk was just banter. I didn't—"

She raised her hand to stop him. "It wasn't the spy talk, Tom. It was saying we were going to spend the night together."

"I may come on strong at times, but I couldn't proposition a woman an hour after I met her—no matter how beautiful she was."

"Thanks for the left-handed compliment, but I'm afraid you did exactly that."

"Are you sure you didn't—"

"Do the words 'I'm going to spend the night with you' sound familiar?"

"I didn't say night; I said evening. I'm going to spend the evening with you."

"You said night."

"I meant evening." His expression was a blend of embarrassment and enjoyment. "It's a good thing

Freud's not still alive—think about the field day the good doctor could have with a slip like that one.''

You're out of practice, Powers. Loosen up. "I may have overreacted."

"My internal censor must have been out to lunch."

"I accept your apology."

"I haven't offered one. Actually, I like my first, uncensored suggestion better."

They started threading their way toward the museum's exit.

"Have pity on me and apologize so I don't have to dwell on the fact that I defended my honor like a mid-Victorian spinster." She ignored the fact that he'd propositioned her a second time.

"Are you a spinster?"

She noticed his quick glance at her left hand. No clues there: The telltale wedding ring stripe had finally faded about six months ago. "Divorced."

"Recently?"

"It became final a year ago. And you?"

"Single."

She'd expected him to do at least five minutes on the pleasures of perennial bachelorhood or the dangers inherent in marriage, but he did neither. In fact, some of his high spirits seemed to fade. Interesting.

They exited the other side of the Open Air Museum. If possible, the crowd seemed even denser here. Families spread out beach blankets on the sidewalk and set up folding chairs in order to view the spectacular bonfire and fireworks over Mount Myojo that would begin in just over an hour.

Next to her, Tom whistled. "We should've made reservations. Think it's too late to call Ticketron?"

Katie glanced around as another patch of viewing space was snapped up by a young couple with two children dressed in matching white sunsuits. The younger child was no more than three, a chubby round-cheeked girl whose eager smile made Katie swallow hard around memories.

Reflexively she snapped herself back to the present.

"Come on," she said to Tom, pointing to some curb space that hadn't yet been claimed. "We'd better stake out a spot while we still can."

"Reserve a table for two. I'll get us some Pepsis from the stand I saw near the museum." His smile was back. "You did say you wanted to drown yourself in Pepsi, didn't you?"

She settled down on the curb, arranging the skirt of her sundress demurely over her knees. "Trying to bribe me with soda, Yankee?"

"I'm a desperate man. Chocolate bars, silk stockings—anything for an interpreter."

Tom pushed back into the crowd in search of Pepsi in the land of sake and green tea, while Katie sat on the curb and did her level best to keep from watching the little girl with the happy smile who reminded Katie of all she'd lost when her own child had died.

It didn't seem possible, but the crowds had doubled while Tom was at the snack bar. Men, women and children occupied every available square foot of space and even the lower branches of some trees that lined the street. And it felt as if everyone's gaze was firmly focused on him as he threaded his way back through the throng, balancing his provisions.

A group of young girls in jeans and tank tops giggled as he walked by and called out something that he could only assume was the Japanese equivalent of "Hey, baby!"

His sense of direction was bad enough; with all of his landmarks covered with beach blankets and bodies and picnic coolers, he'd be lucky if he found Katie before his next birthday.

However, searching for a red-haired woman in a black-haired society brought with it certain intrinsic benefits. Even in the gathering darkness, her wavy hair blazed like a forest fire. All he had to do was walk toward the flames.

"I was getting worried about you," Katie said, taking the soda cans from him as he finally sat down next to her on the curb. "Any problems?"

"None that a crash course in Japanese wouldn't have cured. I think I paid forty-six dollars for two Pepsis and a Hershey bar."

"I hope you're kidding."

"I think I am, but I'm not sure. I couldn't understand the counter clerk, so I finally handed over a pile of yen and told the clerk to take what I owed."

"Are you always that trusting?"

"It's not that I'm so trusting, Katie. It's that I was so desperate." He told her what the counter clerk had taken and how many coins he had received back in change.

"My faith in human nature is restored. You found an honest man."

"Honest woman," he corrected her, enjoying the subtle lifting of her left eyebrow.

"That explains it. She simply couldn't resist your all-American charm."

"You sound cynical, Ms. Powers." He couldn't quite figure the expression in her lovely blue eyes.

"Not cynical. Realistic. How many clerks back home would have dealt honestly with a benighted tourist?"

"I like to think most would."

"Then you're a dreamer, Tom."

"I'll take that as a compliment."

He watched her as she took a long sip of her soda. He liked the way her cheekbones looked as she drew in on the straw, the way her mouth glistened with moisture. Hell, she was a pleasure to look at no matter what she was doing.

He forced himself not to stare at her; instead, he looked up at the mountain where a letter from the Japanese alphabet had been carved into the side. Precisely at 8:00 p.m., the lights of the town would go out and the outlined letter, symbol for the word "great," would be ignited by hundreds of torches springing to life simultaneously. Then the late summer sky would bloom with *hanabi*—the pyrotechnics the Japanese were justly famous for.

"How do you manage to keep your innocence in a big, bad city like Las Vegas?" Katie asked, putting the soda can down next to her on the curb.

"It's not that big or that bad," he answered. "We go to work and school and the supermarket just like everyone else. You can pick the life-style you want; no one grabs you and forces you into Caesar's or the Golden Nugget."

"No topless bank tellers?"

"Just the occasional topless mail carrier."

"Have you lived there all your life?"

"I was born in Elko, up north, but my father brought the business down to Vegas when I was three. It's been home for as long as I can remember." They were skirting painful territory. He took a swig of soda and wished it were scotch.

"I guess your father is holding down the fort while you're out spying on the competition?"

"My father died a year and a half ago."

She flinched—a slight movement of her slender shoulders—however, she didn't mouth the obligatory "I'm sorry," and he was glad. He'd heard enough of that after the accident to last ten lifetimes.

He drew his hand through his hair and smiled at her. "Maybe we should just exchange bios and be done with it."

"You should have told me to mind my own business."

"You would have been insulted."

"Not at all. I hate nosy people. I had no business being one."

"It was a logical question. Unfortunately, it was one with a lousy answer." He reached over and took her hand. "No harm done." He could feel the hesitation in the way her slender fingers rested tentatively against his. "Of course, you understand this means I get to question you at length about your own life: profession, income, tax status—"

Laughter broke through her restraint. The fullness of the sound, the richness, delighted him.

"You'll do anything to hang on to your interpreter, won't you?"

"Am I that transparent?"

"An open book, Sagan."

He squeezed her hand and she returned the pressure. A tingling sensation rippled along his spine. Through the scent from unfamiliar flowers and trees carried on the evening breeze, he caught the faint smell of Shalimar on her skin that he'd first noticed on the train, and some vivid sexual images popped into his head unbidden.

This time he couldn't blame the altitude.

Katie couldn't help thinking, *You're perverse, Powers, totally perverse.*

Tom wasn't the only one Sigmund Freud would have had a field day with—some of the thoughts leaping through Katie's brain would have provided material for quite a few juicy treatises.

When Dr. Freud had asked, "What do women want?" he was just one of many over the years who were hard-pressed to come up with an answer. Katie was finding it pretty difficult herself.

When Tom had said, "I'm going to spend the night with you," she'd reacted with maidenly zeal and stormed off in a self-righteous huff. It wasn't so much indignation that had prompted her melodramatic retreat; it was self-defense. She'd suddenly realized that she was about to say yes.

There was something infinitely seductive about being strangers in a strange land. New scents, new sounds, the intimacy forged by common language in a land of uncommon beauty. How easy it would be to cast off the chains of expectation and disappointment and simply enjoy what is, without worrying about what was or what will be. How tempting.

From some unseen place came the strains of Japanese music, dissonant to her Western ears, but oddly lovely. The music added to the feeling of unreality sweeping over her. "I guess we're not in Kansas anymore."

"Katie?"

She blinked and looked at Tom. "Sorry. I think it finally hit me—just how far away from home we really are."

He smiled, and she could see his teeth gleaming white in the gathering darkness. "There's no place like home?"

"Home is fine," Katie said, "but right now I'm happy where I am."

"You're not going to click your heels three times and disappear on me?"

"And leave Oz just before show time? Not even the Wizard himself could make me do that."

Her voice faded and she realized the crowd around them had fallen silent. Even the music had stopped. Only the sounds of collective breathing and rustling papers marred the stillness.

The quiet, however, carried with it an intensity, a sense of expectation, that was almost palpable. She and Tom drew closer together, their fingers interlocking.

Magic and miracles were in the air all around them, and it wasn't difficult for Katie to believe that the spirits of the beloved dead were indeed afoot, waiting for the torchlight that would guide their way back to heaven once again.

Foreign though the custom was, she found it easy to understand the comfort taken from it.

Next to her, Tom Sagan was quiet, deep within his own thoughts. She stole a look at him in the darkness, and her breath caught at the clean lines of his profile. His strong jaw was in rugged counterpoint to the perfection of his features, saving him from plastic matinee-idol handsomeness.

She was drifting into pleasant fantasy when the lights of the town blinked, then went out. The darkness was all-encompassing and she was very happy to be next to Tom. He squeezed her hand once, as if he understood and shared her thoughts, and she smiled.

From somewhere in the crowd behind her, a child's cry, high and clear, pierced the stillness; then, before the sound blended with the night, the design in the side of the mountain leaped to life, ablaze with a wild and primitive fire whose flames threatened to reach down and ignite her soul.

The crowd, contemplative before, turned celebratory. Parents embraced their children; elderly men and women watched the mountain as if they could see the spirits ascending toward heaven; lovers kissed beneath the cloak of darkness. Cries of *"Banzai!"* filled the air.

The emotions released were as elemental as the fire, as timeless as the night. Katie was swept away on memories of her child, and of the dreams that had died with her.

But tonight, the memories weren't sad.

For the first time, she felt part of something larger, some force that encompassed both the ebb and the flow of life, something that promised continuity and renewal. The mountain fires burned hot enough to begin melting the ice she'd carried in her heart for so long.

"Godspeed," she said softly. "Godspeed, Jill."

Tom had been choreographing the Ogatsu family's upcoming fireworks display in his mind while waiting for the maroons, the aerial report that was the traditional opener of a fireworks show.

While he understood the tradition behind the Daimonji Yaki, he hadn't expected the lighting of the ritual torches on the mountainside to be anything but a rather staid preamble to the main event: the glittering, unbridled, magnificent display of pyrotechnical genius.

He was wrong.

The moment the mountainside blazed to life, Tom was filled with the strangest combination of emotions imaginable: exhilaration, sorrow and hope exploded inside him, going off like a barrage of Saturn rockets.

For the first time since the accident that took his father and fiancée eighteen months ago, he felt he was on the right road, that the destination he had chosen would lead him out of guilt and despair and back into the light.

Bringing that trophy back to Sagan Fireworks would prove once and for all time that he had it in him to persevere, that the days of taking the easy road, searching for shortcuts, were gone. That what had happened hadn't been his fault at all.

It was all waiting for him right here.

The key to winning the contest back in Las Vegas one month from now would soon be lighting up the skies over Hakone. The one element missing in his previous attempts at transcending the spectacular and achieving the miraculous was there for the taking. All he had to do was watch and wait.

Around him, the crowd erupted. Their shouts of joy mixed with the pagan beauty of the mountainside, and he let loose with a yell of his own, a visceral cry from the heart. Adrenaline ripped through his body and made him feel invincible.

He was eager to share his elation. He turned to Katie just in time to hear the word "Godspeed." Just in time to see the tears poised below her beautiful eyes.

"Katie?"

She turned and looked at him.

The look in her eyes matched the feeling in his heart. He drew her into his arms and let the scent of her perfume fill his head with dreams.

It happened so naturally that Katie had no time to worry about propriety; being in Tom Sagan's arms seemed as inevitable as the next beat of her heart.

And when he lowered his mouth toward hers and she felt her lips part beneath his, she was caught up in the wild magic of the moment in a way that was as terrifying as it was unavoidable.

How well she had kept her heart hidden in Boston; how well she had guarded her solitude.

How foolish it all seemed now.

One of Tom's hands was behind her head, and the feel of his strong fingers at the base of her neck added to her excitement. She placed her right hand on his chest, just above the opening of his white cotton shirt, so that her palm rested on his warm, smooth flesh. His heart pounded beneath her hand.

The kiss deepened as his tongue slid across her teeth and plunged—

She couldn't stop the laughter and, thank God, neither could Tom. The first explosion of fireworks overhead literally shook the ground beneath them.

"Remember this date," Tom said as they pulled apart, bathed in the glow of the silver fireworks. "I've been waiting for thirty-two years to feel the earth move."

Katie was laughing so hard that tears slid down her cheeks. "I don't think we can take any credit for that, Tom." Another series of explosions rocked the cheering crowd as she covered her ears for a moment. "I think the fireworks have something to do with it."

"If you don't tell, I won't," Tom said, his eyes twinkling. "No one has to know it took the Ogatsus' Ten Thousand Thunders to make it happen."

"The secret's safe with me."

A high-pitched whirring noise sounded over the mountain, but it wasn't followed by a display.

"That's a Mad Lion," Tom said. "Ogatsu uses it to signal the second portion of the show."

"Aha! So we *did* make the earth move, after all."

"Sorry to disappoint you, Katie, but what shook us up was just the salute. They use it to invigorate the crowd before the real displays go off."

"Such a scholarly approach."

"When you talk about an artist like Ogatsu, it is."

Tom explained about tension, relaxation and elegance, and the master Japanese pyrotechnician illustrated those concepts in the night sky with perfect chrysanthemums whose petals flashed with brilliance, graceful willows whose tendrils trailed down the side of the mountain, and autumn cherry blossoms so distinct, Katie could almost smell the sweet fragrance.

The sky exploded with color, sliding through the spectrum from cool turquoise and green and silver to the burning intensity of crimson and amber and gold. A bouquet of peonies wreathed the mountain, followed by a cascade of willows that bloomed in tiers like a flowering Niagara.

It was flash and fire and beauty, and as far removed from the rockets and sparklers of Katie's childhood as to seem mystical. A particularly effective lily brought the crowd roaring to its feet. The combination of noise and splendor had raised Katie's expectations to a fever pitch.

Tom leaned over toward her left ear so he could be heard over the din. "If I'm reading his choreography right, this should be the finale."

Finale? The only way Katie could imagine this performance being topped was if Ogatsu could call on Venus and Saturn to join in the show.

She was wrong. Unbelievably, they had saved the best for last.

Boom!
Bang!
Crash!

One after another, shells firing so rapidly that they seemed simultaneous, the sky filled with stars of silver and gold, spreading from the horizon clear to the heavens.

When the show finally ended, and the sky was graced only with the moon and the Milky Way, it seemed strangely barren.

"I had no idea," she murmured. "I'm properly awed."

"And I'm starved," he said, taking her arm and helping her up from the curb. He seemed restless. For a moment she thought she saw sadness in his eyes, but it quickly disappeared when he smiled. "Would you care to have dinner with me?"

"I'd love to, but I'm meeting Gwen at the hotel by the station. We were going to have dinner and go back to Tokyo in the morning."

"I'm sorry to hear it."

"Don't be sorry," Katie said, touching his forearm with her hand. "You're welcome to join us."

"This time, Katie, three is definitely a crowd."

"Gwen won't mind. She—" Katie stopped. "Do you think we'll have trouble getting reservations?"

The look on his face was enough to buckle her knees. "I want to spend the night with you, Katie," he said, pulling her into his arms. "And this time I mean exactly what I'm saying."

3

Katie tried to ignore the way his body felt against hers.

"You just want to keep your interpreter," she said lightly. "You're afraid you'll get on the wrong train and end up in Taiwan instead of Tokyo tonight."

"Good try, Katie." His breath tickled her ear. "You'll have to come up with a better answer than that."

"There is no better answer than that," she mumbled. She wanted to say yes, but after seven years of marriage, she had not yet mastered her new single freedom.

She knew she should say no, but denying herself what promised to be pleasure of the first order seemed almost sacrilegious. Sidestepping the issue with graceful humor was obviously the best way to go.

Unfortunately, Tom Sagan was too blunt—or too determined—for that approach to work. "We've already made the earth move without even trying," he said. "Think of what we can do if we put our minds to it."

She couldn't keep the laughter from her voice. "Don't be greedy, Sagan. We've already accomplished something it took the post-Hemingway generation thirty years to decide could never be done.''

"Why not start our own legend? Give the yuppies something new to aspire to.''

"Yuppies have enough on their hands searching for the perfect tortellini," Katie said. "I'd hate to add to their burden."

"You're not a yuppie yourself? Since you're from Boston, I kind of wondered if—"

"Don't even say it! I want more out of my future than CDs and a low resting heart rate.''

He touched her cheek gently with one finger. "What do you want out of your future, Katie Powers? What is it you're looking for?''

"Dinner would be nice, for starters," she said, moving regretfully from his embrace. "You're starving, in case you've forgotten.''

"I haven't forgotten, Katie.''

She liked the easy way he accepted her decision without pressing the point with a display of latent macho aggression. Her few forays into the singles world since her divorce from Robert Morrison had been eye-opening, to say the least. Apparently there were still a few exceptions.

"Gwen said the restaurant at the hotel near the Cho-koku no Mori station is first-class," Katie said. "I wish you'd join us.''

Say yes, Tom. The night was too special, the attraction between them too exquisite, to let it end.

"You're a cruel woman, Katie.''

But before she could say another word, he bent down and kissed her with a combination of such sweetness, such sensuality, that her body moved into his embrace of its own volition.

She didn't dare look into his eyes. If she did, there would be no way she could hide the way she wanted him.

There would be no way she could refuse.

Katie wanted him as much as he wanted her. When she moved into his arms like that, only a fool or a child would have believed otherwise, and Tom Sagan was neither.

However, there was no denying the fact that she wasn't about to give in to her yearnings, and he wasn't about to push. Anything he could say to convince her that what had happened between them minutes ago had rocked his foundation just as it had rocked hers would sound like a transparent ploy to lure a reluctant woman to his bed.

She would never believe him. And if she did believe him, it was sure to scare the hell out of her.

Maybe as much as it was scaring the hell out of him.

"Come on." He reluctantly broke off the kiss. "Let's go to dinner, Katie Powers."

Let's go to dinner before I end up making you the appetizer, entrée and dessert.

By 10:00 P.M. they were on their third drink, and the elusive Gwen Powers Mifune had yet to make her appearance.

"I don't think you have a sister." Tom popped another exotic but unidentifiable appetizer into his mouth. "I think you're an only child with a vivid imagination."

"When I was a teenager, I wished I were one," Katie said. Smiling was becoming more of an effort. "I have a sister, Tom. I just don't know where she is."

"Are you sure she said to meet you in this hotel? Maybe there's another one near the station."

"Thanks for trying, but I'm sure this is the one. She told me to look for the small waterfall in the lobby near the check-in desk."

"Maybe she got here early, decided to take a room and fell asleep."

"I doubt if—"

"It's worth a shot, isn't it?"

Katie slid out of the small booth they'd been sharing in the bar off the main dining room. Tom threw a pile of yen down on the table to cover the bar tab, and she plucked two 500-yen notes out of the pile and pressed them back into his hand.

"No tipping in Japan," she said. "It's included in the charge."

"I probably could finance a second car with the tips I've been leaving," he said as he followed her to the main lobby and the registration desk. "Where were you when I needed you?"

The young female clerk in charge of check-ins spoke English haltingly but happily, and was clearly delighted at the chance to practice it on Katie.

"I have message for you, Miss Powers," she said, handing a folded piece of paper to Katie. "You will please to call that number."

Katie must have looked as frightened as she felt, because Tom put an arm around her shoulders. If it was Hiro's number at the hospital she would—

It was Gwen's home number.

"I'll strangle her!"

Tom removed his arm from her shoulder. "Katie?"

"She's still home. I can't believe this! She forgot all about meeting me."

She could tell by the twitching of his mustache that Tom was having a difficult time keeping a straight face.

"Laugh and I'll kill you, too, Sagan. This isn't funny."

He did an admirable job of restraining his emotions, but the twinkle in his eyes gave him away.

"I'm beginning to see a pattern emerging, Ms. Powers. Overreacting isn't an occasional thing—it's a way of life."

She chose to ignore him and concentrated instead on digging up some ten-yen coins from the bottom of her canvas bag. What the hell was the code for Tokyo? 03? 04?

Gwen picked the phone up on the first ring and Katie was off and running.

"Do I get a chance to defend myself," Gwen said, "or is this a trial without jury?"

"You're lucky there's a trial at all," Katie said, turning away from Tom's amused expression. "You should be shot on sight. Where in hell are you, sister dearest?"

"The trains are out until morning. I was half expecting you to show up at my doorstep. You must have been on the last train to get through. The railway office said—"

"That a piece of rail became embedded in the undercarriage of a train. I was on that train. Just tell me where I can get a bus and—"

"There is no bus until morning."

"A taxi?"

"Not tonight."

"A hotel room?" This wasn't really happening to careful, cautious Katie Powers, was it?

"Katie, believe me, I called every hotel in the area. They're all packed to the rafters because of the holiday."

"This isn't funny, Gwen. If this is some twisted plan of yours to blast me out of my rut, so help me, I'll—"

"I feel terrible about this, Katie. I even tried to reach Hiro at his conference. I thought maybe one of his friends could drive me out there, but by the time I'd get to you, you'd be on the train for Tokyo."

Tom had been discreetly eavesdropping before. He was listening openly now.

"So what am I supposed to do now, big sister? Sleep on the sidewalk?"

"You don't have to yell at me, Katie. I can hear you."

"You got me into this mess, Gwen. The least you can do is figure a way out of it. Being stuck here alone—"

"Alone?" Tom said. "Thanks a lot, Katie. And after we felt the earth move..."

"Who's that?" Gwen asked. "What are you up to?"

"I'm not up to anything," Katie said, "and don't change the subject."

"I heard a man's voice! You didn't pick someone up at the festival, did you?" The note of disbelief in Gwen's voice did nothing to mollify Katie.

"No, I did not pick someone up at the festival," Katie practically shouted into the phone.

"It was on the train," Tom said. "You picked me up on the train."

Katie glared at him. "I was minding my own business, if you remember. If anyone did any picking up, it was you with that idiotic spy story."

"Don't stop now," Gwen said. "This is getting interesting."

"Mind your own business," Katie snapped.

"You don't have to get nasty," Tom said.

"I was talking to my sister."

"You shouldn't speak to your sister like that. It's not her fault the tracks are down."

"I like this man," Gwen said. "Who is he?"

"James Bond," Katie said. "He's here on assignment."

"What does he look like?"

"He's five-two, has buck teeth and wears glasses. Women swoon at the sight of him."

"That's slander," Tom said. "I could sue you for that."

"He sounds tall," Gwen said.

"He's not."

"He also sounds sexy."

"Forget it, Gwen."

Tom's ear was pressed close to the receiver. Katie tried to push him away.

"What did he mean, 'we felt the earth move'?" A new note of sisterly concern crept into Gwen's voice. "Katie, when I said live dangerously, I didn't mean—"

Tom laughed. "Tell her, Katie. Tell her how we made the earth move."

The last shred of Katie's control snapped. "Here," she said, pushing the phone against his chest. "Tell her yourself!"

Tom stared as Katie stormed across the lobby and out the door.

"Is anybody there?"

He put the phone to his ear. "Gwen?"

"Yes. Is this James Bond?"

"Alias Tom Sagan."

"You're not five-two, are you?"

"Add a foot. Is she always so temperamental?"

"Afraid so. I suppose she's standing there in a snit."

"Afraid not. She left."

"What?" Gwen's voice escalated in volume.

"She shoved the phone into my chest and walked out."

"Oh, my God! The streets are crazy tonight with the festival."

He hadn't thought of that. "Are you sure the trains are down?"

"Positive. First one back is at five twenty-two a.m."

"And no room at the inn?"

"I was going to ask you if you had a suite of rooms with one to spare for a hot-tempered redhead."

"Sorry. I was going back to Tokyo myself."

"Tom, would you catch up with her? If anything happened to her there, I'd never forgive myself."

Gwen quickly told him of a restaurant that would be open until the wee hours in celebration of the festival.

They said goodbye and he was about to hang up and race outside to look for Katie. "I'll keep my eye on her." Tough duty.

"Thanks," Gwen said. "Maybe you can come over for drinks one night before Katie leaves. I'm dying to know how you two made the earth move."

"It certainly took you long enough," Katie said when Tom found her sitting on a marble bench near the front door of the hotel. "I could have been swept away into life as a geisha by now."

"Geishas are sweet and subservient. You'd last about fifteen minutes."

"I hope you and Gwen had a great conversation." They should have—they had been on the phone long enough.

He rubbed the spot on his chest where she'd jammed the telephone receiver. "Terrific. She told me how to heal a broken rib."

Katie's breath drew in sharply. "I didn't mean to hurt you, Tom. I was just so damned angry that I—"

"Overreacted," he cut in. "I think we've been there before, Katie. Next time I'll be prepared."

"There won't be a next time. Believe it or not, I don't make a habit of losing my temper."

"Can't prove it by me, Ms. Powers." He glanced down at his watch. "I've only known you seven and a half hours and I've seen you explode three times."

"Your fireworks may be great but your arithmetic is terrible," Katie said. "I admit my temper may have gotten away from me once or twice—" she ignored Tom's ill-concealed laugh "—but *three* times?" She shook her head. "That requires proof, Sagan."

"The train station when I made that Freudian slip," Tom said. "Back there in the hotel with your sister."

"And that's it," Katie interrupted. "Two minor outbursts. I can hardly be blamed for—"

"You're forgetting the telephone in the rib cage."

"Three times," Katie said. "I can't believe it."

"Three times."

"I apologize."

"Apology accepted."

"I don't suppose you'd believe me if I said I never lose my temper?"

Tom arched a brow. "Would you believe it?"

She had to smile. "Probably not, but it's true. Back home I'm cool and collected."

"Maybe it's the altitude here."

"That's your excuse. I'll have to come up with a new one."

Tom sat down on the bench next to her. "I always thought redheads were temperamental."

"I suppose you believe in the Tooth Fairy, too?"

He covered his ears. "Please! Not all my illusions in the same day."

"I actually have a reputation for being very reasonable and levelheaded."

He laughed out loud. "Maybe in Boston, Katie. You're going to have to hire a PR firm to convince me of that."

"I don't think Bob and I had three real fights in seven years."

"Bob?" She could sense the quickening of interest beneath Tom's casual question.

"My ex-husband. He's a lawyer back home in Boston." Why on earth had she brought him into the conversation?

"Maybe that's one reason he's your ex-husband. Fighting can be good for the soul."

She thought about the calm, friendly emptiness of their years together, and the way the death of their baby daughter had exposed that emptiness for what it was. "I don't think fighting would have made any difference."

"Was it another woman?"

She shook her head.

"Another man?"

"Bob is remarried and the father of a baby girl."

"That's not what I meant."

She reddened. "I don't play around."

"So you told me earlier."

She raised a fist and held it under Tom's nose. "If you value the rest of your ribs, you'll put this subject to rest."

He covered her fist with his hand. "Explosion number four. I'm going to need a calculator to keep track, Katie."

Katie was about to say something light and breezy but her eyes met Tom's and the words died in her throat. Mesmerized, she watched as he raised her hand to his mouth and pressed his lips against her clenched fist. Her fingers opened like a night flower as her body swayed toward him.

He stood up and she rose with him, her hand still captured by his.

"Come with me," he said, drawing her near his side.

"Where?" The word was a whisper from her lips.

"I can't believe I'm saying this, but I think it's time we had dinner."

Hunger, fine and magnificent, rose within her, and it had nothing to do with a need for sustenance. The need within her went deeper than the bone, beyond the moment. Freudian slip or not, if he were to ask her again...

But there was no room at the inn—neither the Sheraton nor the Hilton nor the Chokoku no Mori Hotel had any place for two lovers to play with fire.

They went in search of dinner instead.

4

The kimono-clad waitress bowed, then hurried away toward the kitchen to bring back a fourth plate of spaghetti and tomato sauce.

Tom waited until the young woman was out of earshot. "I think we shocked her."

"I don't think we shocked her," Katie said, "but I'll bet we've given the chef something to talk about." She poured some more Kirin into his glass and then her own. "I don't think they get too many requests for linguini and clam sauce."

The ends of his mustache tilted in a smile. "Hell, I couldn't believe they had spaghetti. It was worth a shot, wasn't it?"

They'd been sitting for nearly two hours in the tiny restaurant tucked at the foot of a mountain. Groups of festival revelers had come and gone. Tired families stranded by the train drooped over the low tables near the front, while the kids sprawled out on blankets against the wall.

Under normal circumstances, Katie would have been sprawled out on one of those blankets herself, but right now she felt pumped full of adrenaline; every cell in her body tingled with awareness of her surroundings—and of Tom.

She felt as if someone had opened the door to a secret passageway and she had stepped through, leaving her Boston self behind.

Who would have figured that midnight would find her sitting in a Japanese restaurant near Mount Myojo, eating spaghetti with a man from Las Vegas who made fireworks for a living? Twenty-four hours ago she would have laughed at the possibility. Now she was beginning to think anything was possible.

They talked about fireworks and the Japanese connection to art while Tom polished off his third entrée.

"Do you think I should ask if they have biscuit tortoni?"

"Why don't we settle for plain ice cream instead?"

"What's the matter, Katie Powers? Don't you know the Japanese words for biscuit tortoni?"

She laughed. "Smart man, Sagan. You catch on quickly."

The waitress brought them ice cream and a pot of steaming green tea.

"I think you know enough about fireworks right now to start up your own company," Tom said. "Sorry I monopolized things."

"Don't be sorry. I loved it. It's not every day you get the facts from an expert."

"When we met on the train, you said you were here for pleasure and business." The look he gave her was assessing. "I know about the pleasure. What's the business?"

"Tech writing. I specialize in those horrid little 'attach part A to part B and pray' manuals you find stuck in with your toaster and your stereo."

"Somebody writes them? I thought they were part of a sinister Communist plot to undermine the sanity of the Free World."

"Sorry. I'm responsible."

"I bought my cousin a bicycle for Christmas and it took me until her birthday last month to get the damned thing together."

"This time I'm innocent." She laughed at the scowl on his handsome face. "I don't do bicycles. I can only be blamed for appliances, sound systems and computer manuals."

"Do you free-lance, or do a group of you sit around, rubbing your hands together in glee, trying to come up with new ways to drive the rest of us crazy?"

"Both." She named the famous Boston-based conglomerate she used to work for. "Now I free-lance."

He seemed impressed. "You left to start your own company?"

Ouch. "I was fired."

"You said put part A in part Z?"

"The department head put part A, design plans, into part B, the hands of the competition. It was an ugly situation, and it ended up with everyone in the department getting a pink slip."

He polished off the rest of the ice cream. "How long ago was that?"

"Four months, five days—I can't tell you how many hours because of the time change."

"You miss it."

"You might say that." A short, bitter laugh broke through. "I'd been with them for nine years."

Her nine-to-five life had been one of the few things she'd been able to count on during a very rocky period following her divorce, when friends were in short supply.

"The free-lance work isn't going well?"

"Actually, it's going quite well. I have eight steady clients, and I may pick up a contract from an import firm in Tokyo that needs someone to write copy for the back of its cosmetics packages."

"Sounds great to me. So what's the problem?" He was still smiling that great smile of his, but she could tell he sensed the tension beneath her words.

"Security," she said. "I'm used to security."

"Like a husband?"

"Like a regular paycheck with sick leave and paid vacations."

"Sounds boring."

"Not to me."

"Are you sure about that?"

She hesitated a moment too long. "Of course I'm sure. I like knowing that every Friday a big, fat paycheck will be coming in."

"And do you like knowing that thirty years from now, you'll still be at the same desk, waiting for the same big, fat Friday paycheck?"

It sounded disgusting, but Katie wasn't about to admit to that. "Not all of us have the entrepreneurial instinct, Tom."

"If you're making money and bringing in new clients after only four months of free-lancing, then you've got the instinct, Katie."

"Be quiet, Tom," she said. "My ice cream's melting."

He managed to pick up the conversation right where they left off as they left the restaurant and started walking back toward the hotel near the Chokoku no Mori train station.

"Four months isn't enough time to gauge your success," he said as they carefully stepped around a man sleeping near the curb. "As long as you can pay your bills, you should give it at least a year."

"Actually, I've been considering a job offer I received before I left Boston."

Her ex-husband, Bob, was an attorney for a large electronics firm that needed the services of an experienced and talented tech writer. She had free-lanced for Bernstein, Jameson and Coulter during her marriage. They had liked her work and she had liked their attitude.

The money offer was superb, the benefits were incomparable and the work was deadly dull.

"Back to a nice, comfortable routine?"

She glanced up at him. "You sound like my sister."

"Up every morning at six, hit the freeway by seven, take an hour lunch, then commute back home through traffic." He shook his head. "And all that for profit-sharing. Doesn't sound too appealing, does it?"

"No, it doesn't." Suddenly the thought of a life neatly packaged in a pin-striped suit sounded stultifying.

"Give yourself a chance, Katie," Tom said, his voice low. "Why fence yourself in when you can run free?"

"Did Gwen tell you to say that?"

"All Gwen told me was where to find a restaurant."

"You haven't known me well enough to psychoanalyze me, Sagan."

"Maybe you forgot to put your defenses up tonight, Katie."

The oppressive heat of a Japanese summer day had given way to the silky breezes of a summer night, made even more intoxicating by the scent of exotic flowers and the night cries of wild birds in the distance.

Boston and reality seemed a galaxy away.

Maybe Tom was right.

Maybe tonight was the night to leave her defenses down and live dangerously.

From earliest childhood, Tom had been trained to notice and remember details. Despite his wild and rebellious nature, he'd quickly understood that survival in a fireworks compound depended upon being a good judge of character, thinking fast and noticing everything that went on around you.

So it wasn't hard for him to detect the sadness behind Katie's impossibly blue eyes, or the reined-in restlessness visible despite her best attempts at concealing it.

Maybe in Massachusetts she was known as quiet, levelheaded Katie Powers, but the woman he'd met that afternoon was as full of fire and light as the sky over the Hakone Mountain Range a few hours ago.

And even more beautiful.

They were following a narrow road that curved around a small lake. The air smelled of salt and wet grass, and he leaned closer to Katie to catch the sweet scent of her perfume. A slight wind blew up, and he used it as an excuse to put his arm around her and feel the warm, soft skin of her shoulder against his hand.

This was a moment out of time, as unreal and fleeting as the golden comets and glittering cascades of stars he fashioned for a burst of beauty in the lonely night.

He wanted to forget that dawn would come and, with it, a return to reality and responsibility and debts yet unpaid. Once he'd been expert at running away from reality; now it seemed to hold him captive.

Katie offered him a chance to dream again.

"I'm glad we met, Katie Powers."

Why not put it right on the line? Their time was limited, and Tom had never mastered the art of subtlety.

"Three plates of spaghetti and you're a happy man."

"That's not what I'm talking about."

"I didn't think so." In the darkness her expression was unreadable.

"Remember what I said before about Fate?" he asked. Katie nodded. "Do you still think I'm way off base?"

"No," she whispered. "Not at the moment."

He stopped walking, and she turned to look at him. She shimmered in the moonlight, her fiery red hair tempered with a silvery glow.

For months, nothing—and no one—had been able to sway him from his course. He'd come to Japan with one goal in mind: to discover how to take Sagan Fireworks over the top.

Katie Powers in her blue-and-white sundress was a detour he hadn't planned on, a trip he hadn't expected to take again.

Pleasure for the moment had its place; he had had his share of momentary passion and gone on with nothing more than a fond memory.

This was something different.

Katie with her fine mind and sharp tongue and uncommon beauty offered nothing, but promised the world. Her passions were banked, her emotions kept on a short lead.

And he couldn't help but wonder how it would feel to be the one to run with her when she finally broke free.

Don't ask, Katie thought. *Just take me in your arms and kiss me.*

Something was happening between them, something magical and inexplicable, and words would only break the fragile spell. Whether it was Fate or Lady Luck or Karma, she didn't know.

The only thing she was certain of was that she was far, far away from home and falling in love.

He was just watching her, those marvelous golden eyes of his focused on her face as if she held the secrets of the universe.

No more than a foot separated them. How easy it would be to take that step and end the exquisite tension that crackled between them, almost visible in the summer darkness.

She hesitated.

He smiled.

She lost her nerve.

He put his arm around her shoulder again and they continued on toward the train station.

Idiot, she thought. *You'll never see him again.*

She wouldn't be meeting him over the watercooler, or catching the sly glances of friends who wondered what really went on between them.

It was entirely safe to fall head over heels in love with him. Once the train rumbled into the station to whisk her back to Tokyo, the relationship would die a natural death. She should have simply walked into his arms and taken her chances.

By the time they reached the hotel, it was after two in the morning. Apparently many other stranded revelers had decided the unair-conditioned lobby of the Cho-koku no Mori Hotel was an excellent spot to spend the night, because every chair, every sofa and every available inch of floor space was occupied.

"I think there's a spot by the telephone banks," Tom said, pointing to a tiny patch of space big enough for a five-year-old. "Why don't you—"

She shook her head. "No, thanks. It's too hot in here. I'd rather stay outside."

"A woman after my own heart."

They walked on toward the train station. A mother and her infant slept on a blanket on a grassy ridge near the station, while a young man guarded them with the fierce devotion of a samurai warrior. Family clusters dotted the roadside, and the sight of the small, soft bundles of sleeping children caused a sharp pain in Katie's heart. Elderly men and women dozed on benches in the waiting room.

Through the dusty window, Katie saw the rich glow of silk robes, the shimmering luster of intricate embroideries. Their traditional clothing provided a strange counterpoint to the Coca-Cola machine near the door, another example of the paradoxical melding of past and present.

"Wait a second, Katie." Tom stopped and rummaged around in his pockets for the right coins for the soda machine.

Katie leaned against the door to the waiting room. Exhaustion crashed over her, and her eyes closed against a wave of dizziness.

"I think you need a jolt of caffeine," Tom said, offering her a can of Coke.

She took a sip. "I'm beyond caffeine. I need twenty-four hours of sleep." The stiff and unyielding tatami mat she'd been sleeping on at Gwen and Hiro's now seemed like a king-size feather bed.

Tom groaned as he led Katie toward an unoccupied patch of grass behind a sleeping family. "Think of me as you crawl between the sheets. I'll be on my way to Kyoto."

"You're not riding back to Tokyo with me?" Amazing how easily disappointment could override fatigue.

"I'm riding back with you, but as soon as we arrive, I'm on another train to Kyoto."

"Don't you have time to go back to your hotel and take a nap?"

"I'll have to sleep on the train. I have a noon appointment."

"Just a one-day trip?" It had to be. He had no luggage.

"I don't know. Depends how things go, I guess."

She nodded and turned away, pretending to stifle a yawn. Reality was approaching with the nearing dawn, and she hated it. She had just three days left in Japan, and the chances of spending one of them with Tom had just evaporated.

You wanted safety and you got it, she thought. Nothing was safer than falling in love with a man who was taking the next train to Kyoto.

Maybe it was his mood, but the area around Tokyo looked suspiciously like New Jersey to Tom as the Bullet train sped toward the station.

If it weren't for the occasional sloping roof of a pagoda nestled along the side of a hill, he would have found it impossible to believe he was so far from home.

Katie was curled up in the next seat to him; she'd been sleeping since they boarded the train at Odawara an hour ago. Tom, unfortunately, hadn't been lucky enough. Not long out of the Chokoku no Mori station, he realized that he couldn't remember one damned thing about the structure of the Ogatsu fireworks display over Hakone a few hours ago. The skinny notebook stashed in his rear pants pocket hadn't been touched. All of the detailed notes he was going to take on timing and color coordination, concussion and glitter had gone up in flames with the lighting of the torches.

Of course, it wasn't a total loss, he thought wryly. He could describe in excruciating detail the way Katie's eyes had sparkled more brightly than the streaking Gold Comets; he knew that Ogatsu's best attempts had fallen far short of duplicating her eyes' rich cobalt blue. He could even call up the memory of the curve of fiery hair against her cheek as she watched the fireworks blazing overhead.

Terrific sensual memories, ones that demanded he spend a hell of a lot more time analyzing them. Katie's cool fire intrigued him; the sadness in her eyes called out to something inside his own soul.

If he hadn't been driven by other memories, other needs, he'd have liked to take his time exploring the magic spell they had both fallen under. He'd meant it that afternoon when he'd said the Fates had had a hand in bringing them together.

Unfortunately, the Fates often displayed a rather ironic sense of timing, and this was no exception. Each time he closed his eyes to let the rocking of the train lull him to sleep, he remembered what had brought him to Japan in the first place.

He remembered why he had come halfway around the world.

Tom had been jumpy that hot June afternoon, but then, he was always jumpy before a show.

"Calm down, son," Buck Sagan had said as they sat down to lunch at Tavern on the Green the day of the Big Apple Extravaganza. "The barges are in place and Eddie has everything under control."

New York City was hosting a two-day country fair, metropolitan style, capped by a fireworks display at the Brooklyn Bridge in Lower Manhattan. Sagan Fireworks had been lucky enough to grab that plum job.

The logistics of it were easy enough: They would float three barges in the East River, and each would be set with shells ready to be fired electronically from the shore.

"I still say you and Paula should be on the last barge," Tom said, ignoring the elegant meal before him. "I'm the only one who doesn't freeze up in front of a television camera."

Paula's high, clear laugh interrupted him. "You're just hoping a talent scout will see you and whisk you off to Hollywood," she said, ruffling his hair. "I can read you like a book, Tommy."

"He's thirty, Paulie," Buck said with a laugh. "Who'd want an old guy like that on the silver screen?"

A few years ago this heavy-duty teasing about his looks would have escalated into a full-scale fight between him and his father. Buck, as steady and dependable as the land that spawned him, couldn't understand the wanderlust and need for excitement that had ruled his son for so long.

Reconciliation had been a long time coming, but since Tom had begun handling the public relations duties for Sagan Fireworks a few years ago, he and Buck had finally grown close.

"You got your mother's looks and your old man's brains for a reason," Buck said to his son. "Now if you pick up some of my future daughter-in-law's business savvy, there'll be no stopping us.''

Paula and Buck began some lightweight bantering and reluctantly Tom let himself be drawn into it, trying to squelch the anxiety that made it difficult to swallow.

Paula sensed his mood and squeezed his hand beneath the linen tablecloth. She had been part of his life for as long as he could remember; through his turbulent adolescence and vagabond early twenties, Paula had been there in his corner.

She had even joined the business before he did. From the start, Paula had been as captivated by the art and science of pyrotechnics as Tom was, and it seemed part of the plans of a very benevolent Fate that she was as important to the future of Sagan Fireworks as any of the born-and-bred Sagans. Their marriage would just make official what had existed in their hearts for a very long time. After years of searching, Tom had finally found all that he needed for happiness.

Spirits that day were high. Sagan Fireworks was beginning to grab more and more of the prestige assignments like the Big Apple Extravaganza, and the future was looking rosy.

Back home in Las Vegas, his mother and Paula's were busy with guest lists and caterers and florists, for this was to be the last major show before the wedding.

The weather reports had initially been iffy, but Fate, his old friend, smiled on him once more and conjured up a clear, crisp evening. The barges were in place, fully loaded and wired with the choreographed shells.

Eddie and Bill would ride number one; his sister Molly and their cousin Frank would ride number two, leaving the third and most important barge for Buck and Paula.

Number three had been a bit tough to set up—there'd been some difficulty getting the shells into the mortar casings, and they'd spent a comical hour racing around Lower Manhattan and the South Street Seaport in search of Vaseline to help wedge the shells in place.

"Maybe you should go out with Buck," Ed Mc-Tavitt said, pulling him aside as the transport boat pulled up to the dock. "I don't like the looks of those shell casings."

Paula had overheard. "Hey, come on, guys!" She flexed her slender arms. "I've been pumping iron in preparation for this. Isn't it time I went out on my maiden voyage?"

Buck was busy talking to the pilot of the barge.

Tom took matters into his own hands and gave Paula a friendly swat on the derriere. "Get going, Paulie," he said. "You've been waiting a long time to go out."

Paula, her dark eyes shining, kissed Tom full on the mouth. She tasted like peppermint.

"You won't be sorry," she whispered in his ear. "When I come back tonight..."

Ed watched as Paula boarded the boat, then muttered something in Tom's direction. Tom ignored the older man.

Going out on the barge held no kick for him. That aspect of the business had long since lost its novelty. For Tom, the real enjoyment was in bringing the pleasure to the public, helping them to understand the facts behind the fun. He hurried to the broadcast booth near the foot of the bridge.

A nagging sense of anxiety curled itself up inside his brain, but he dismissed it as the usual preshow jitters that anyone who dealt with explosives experienced. As soon as the first set of charges went off, he'd settle in.

This time was no exception.

The crowd shrieked its approval as the first series of comets and stars rose from barge one and exploded magnificently over the crest of the majestic old Brooklyn Bridge.

"Sagan Fireworks does it again," the reporter next to Tom said into the microphone. "Another brilliant display!"

A second barrage went up, and cars crossing the bridge blared their horns in spontaneous salute.

Tom relaxed and began to enjoy the give-and-take commentary he and the newscaster from Channel 11 were providing.

The shells loaded on barges one and two performed flawlessly. The night sky glittered with diamond waterfalls and golden sprays of stardust.

"We're coming up onto the finale now," Tom said into the microphone. "You might watch for an enormous bouquet of flowers that—"

He stopped as he felt a vibration building beneath his feet.

What in hell was that?

Sweat broke out under his arms as a crack of manmade thunder split the summer air.

Too soon. God damn it, this shouldn't be happening!

The crowd whistled and applauded madly as the barge itself bloomed like a monstrous multipetaled flower of amber and red.

A blinding flash of magnesium white made Tom shield his eyes.

The air ripped apart with the sound of each explosion and the roar of the crowd.

Stars and comets wheeled off the petals of the flower.

An impossible, never-ending burst of color and heat and sound, more terrifyingly beautiful than anything he'd ever imagined.

"Incredible!" the newscaster screamed. "Incredible! I've never seen anything like this!"

Tom said nothing.

He just sat very still and watched as a sea gull, caught in the wake of a shooting star, glowed silver, then gold, then finally disappeared from sight.

The train slowed as it entered the city limits. Next to him Katie stirred and stretched. She was as beautiful in the morning as she had been at night, and that thought did little to cheer him.

In an hour she'd be heading back to her sister's apartment and he'd be on his way to Kyoto, and whatever it was they'd shared, whatever it was that had almost happened between them, would be just another vacation memory.

Gwen had given him her phone number and address. The slip of paper he'd written it on was tucked away in his rear pocket, but he doubted he'd ever use it.

In a few days, Katie would be heading back home to Boston.

In ten days, he'd be on his way back to Las Vegas, ready to put all he'd learned into motion.

There would be time for nothing else but the competition. Nothing else mattered.

He thought of the way she had felt in his arms.

He wouldn't let anything else matter.

The closer they got to Tokyo, the more distant Tom seemed to grow. By the time the train pulled into the station and they hurried out into the street to hail a cab for Katie, she felt as if the night before had been a dream.

"I'll call you." Tom opened the door of the taxicab for her. "You'll be here until the twentieth. Maybe we can have dinner or something before you leave."

Famous last words.

"If you're back from Kyoto by then, I'd enjoy it." She didn't bother to tell him she'd be leaving the night of the nineteenth.

Again that CinemaScope smile of his. "I'd better be back—I don't have a change of clothes."

She gave the cabdriver, immaculate in a starched white shirt and tie, Gwen's address near St. Luke's International Hospital. Rush hour traffic throbbed all around them.

A return to reality in spades.

"I'll call you," Tom said once again.

"You'd better go. You'll miss your train."

He bent down and kissed her, sharp and sweet, then closed the cab door.

Katie leaned back against the white linen headrest.

"Goodbye, Tom."

The cab lurched into traffic, then wheeled around a corner, and Tom disappeared from sight.

Nice touch, saying you'll call.

It would have been nicer if he'd remembered to take her phone number.

"So why didn't you just give it to him?" Gwen asked later that evening over dinner at a restaurant in the Ginza. "Why do you think you brought one thousand business cards to Tokyo with you?"

"Not to proposition men on the train." Katie picked at her noodles with curry sauce. "If he wanted my number, he should have asked."

"Maybe he forgot."

"Maybe he didn't want it."

"You should have given him your card anyway. If he didn't want it, he'd just toss it away later. No harm done."

"Easy for you to say. It's not your ego that would get trampled."

"Oh, to hell with your ego," Gwen said, loudly enough to draw the attention of some adjacent diners. "Hiro and I wouldn't be married today if I had worried about my ego." She motioned for the waiter to bring them more Pepsi. "Who do you think made the first move?"

"I have no doubt who made the first move, sister dearest. I know you too well."

"You can't sit around waiting for Mr. Right to pop up at your apartment and make a formal introduction, Kaitlin Powers. Sometimes he shows up next to you on a train in Japan."

Katie laughed. "You sound like a hopeless romantic."

"And you sound like a coward."

"We watched fireworks and shared some time together. That's all." *Liar,* she thought.

"I don't believe you."

"Too bad, big sister."

"You should call him," Gwen said.

"I don't know where he's staying."

"There aren't that many Western-style hotels in Kyoto. I doubt if there's more than one Tom Sagan registered in all of Japan."

Don't think it hasn't occurred to me. "Why don't you mind your own business, Gwen? I'm doing fine without your help."

"Doing fine? I don't think sitting home every night is doing fine."

"What should I be doing—hitting the singles bars?"

"You could try dating. Start with your fireworks spy."

"I have tried dating. Once you're over twenty-five, its a highly overrated pastime."

She watched as Gwen took a sip of Pepsi and regrouped her forces.

"Maybe you've been dating the wrong men."

"No 'maybe' about it. They were definitely the wrong men."

"You should be married. You should have a family."

Every muscle in Katie's body went on alert. "Let me be single for a while, Gwen. I enjoy having the bathroom to myself every morning." Her defenses were slipping into place. "I can leave the windows open at night. I don't have to worry about cigarette burns on the end table, or argue over what movie to see on Saturday night."

"You have two and a half bathrooms in your house, Katie, and you never once argued about any of those things with Robert."

True enough. He'd used a separate bathroom, didn't smoke and loved Woody Allen, Steven Spielberg and Louis Malle as much as she did.

"I'm speaking metaphorically, Gwen, and you know it."

"What I know is that you're avoiding the issue."

Katie took a deep breath. "Gwen, don't—"

"It's Robert and Sunny's new baby, isn't it?"

"Don't be ridiculous." Acknowledging the pain would make it twice as difficult to bear.

"He's moved on, Katie." Gwen's voice was soft. "It's time you did, too."

Katie put her chopsticks across her plate. "I sent them flowers and a card, and I'm still alive to tell the tale. I think I'm doing fine."

"The hell you are."

"Why don't you mind your own business, Gwen? Don't you have enough to do without trying to run my life? I'm not ten years old any longer."

Gwen sighed and leaned back in her chair. "You act it, Katie. You still duck your head and look the other way any time anyone even gets close to what you're really thinking. It's all right to mourn Jill, honey. It's normal."

Katie swallowed hard, terrified that she might cry in the middle of the restaurant. "It happened three years ago, Gwen. I've made my peace with it."

"I don't think you have."

Too close. Gwen was cutting too close to the bone.

"Don't turn away from the memories, Katie. Find a way to live with them and start over." Gwen leaned across the small table and patted Katie's arm. "Robert has. You can, too."

Katie nodded. "It's getting late." She rummaged through her pocketbook for the proper currency. "Let me pick up the tab, and we'll go over to Mikimoto so I can drool over all the pearls I can't afford."

"Changing the subject, are you?"

"Very perceptive."

"You hate pearls."

"Not anymore. There's a beautiful pair of pearl-and-diamond earrings in the window that would make a wonderful twenty-ninth birthday present for your favorite younger sister."

Gwen stood up, shaking her head. "My punishment for being pushy?"

"It'll make you think twice next time, won't it?"

"Don't bet on it."

With a little luck, next time, Katie would be safely back home in Boston, and Gwen's lecture would be courtesy of AT&T.

At least then Katie's eyes wouldn't give away the pain.

"She can't be gone," Tom said. "I thought she was here through the twentieth."

Gwen, a pretty and petite blonde with eyes as blue as her sister Katie's, looked up at him. "Afraid not. She left just before midnight on the nineteenth. I'm sorry."

Tom, seated on a narrow sofa obviously not scaled for Western builds, stared at Gwen as if she were speaking Japanese.

"*You're* sorry?" He dragged his hand through his hair. "Why the hell didn't I call her?"

"Good question." Gwen handed him a tall glass of iced tea. "Why didn't you? I gave you the phone number the night you and Katie were at Hakone."

How could he say to Gwen that her sister represented danger, a detour that could keep him from realizing this one last goal that would free him of guilt.

In Kyoto he'd been obsessed, so on fire with the need to absorb anything and everything that could help Sagan Fireworks win the upcoming competition that time had gotten away from him.

A one-day visit had turned into a three-day stay.

His obsession, however, still hadn't managed to keep images of Katie Powers, sexy and intriguing as hell, from popping into his mind at the damnedest moments.

He'd followed her to Tokyo on the chance that the magic hadn't been left on that mountainside.

Face it, Sagan, he thought. *You're in over your head already. You might as well go all the way.*

He handed Gwen his passport and driver's license and American Express card. "I don't have a criminal record," he said, laughing at her expression. "I don't smoke, I drink in moderation and I'm kind to children and small animals. Would you give me Katie's address and phone number in Boston?"

Gwen's eyes twinkled as she handed back his identification. "Tom Sagan, I thought you'd never ask."

5

August 20 Boston

So much for the welcome-home celebration.

Katie closed the heavy door of carved mahogany behind her, took a deep breath of stale, humid air and contemplated taking the next taxi back to Logan Airport.

The only indication that her cleaning service had so much as bothered to show up at her row house in Beacon Hill this past month was the foot-high stack of mail on the rosewood table—and even that was covered with a layer of dust.

Home, sweet home. And not so much as a parakeet to greet her on her return.

She thought of Gwen and Hiro and the wonderful assortment of friends and colleagues they were surrounded with in Tokyo. Her sister had managed to move to the other side of the world and create a network of support for herself, while Katie couldn't manage it right here in the city where she'd been born.

Why hadn't she noticed it before?

She used to blame it on the dissolution of her marriage, on old friends who were unwilling to choose sides and chose to drift away instead.

Losing her job and her old contacts had provided an easy answer, as well.

Now, as she climbed the stairs to her top-floor bedroom, she wondered if maybe—just maybe—some of the blame rested on her own shoulders, on her own natural caution when it came to getting close to someone new.

You didn't have any trouble with Tom Sagan, she thought as she kicked off her shoes inside her bedroom door.

Her highly valued caution hadn't mattered a damn when she had met him on that rickety train and fallen in with his crazy tale of secret operatives and dangerous missions.

Oh, it had been a dangerous mission, all right.

Somehow she'd managed to fall head over heels in love with a man she'd never see again, a man who seemed as unpredictable as she was methodical.

She slipped out of her clothes and slid under the bedcovers.

Maybe it was a good thing she'd never see him again, because no two people on earth could be more dissimilar than Katie Powers and Tom Sagan.

She was logical. He was mercurial.

She believed in order and harmony. He obviously thrived on impulse and disruption.

She was a proper Bostonian and he a born-and-bred Las Vegan.

There was no future for them. The few hours they'd shared together on that magical night were all they'd ever have.

She'd resigned herself to that when he had said goodbye without asking for her phone number.

But as she closed her eyes and drifted toward sleep, there was nothing on earth that could stop her from dreaming about just how interesting life could be with a man who could make the earth move.

August 27 Boston

"No," Tom said, leaning across the blossom-littered counter of the florist's shop. "Put more peonies in the center." He gestured with his hands. "Then stick some more of those white things around the edges."

The clerk, a young brunette woman, sighed loudly enough to be heard back in Tokyo. "The white things, as you call them, are chrysanthemums."

He pointed toward some long-petaled flowers in the display case. "I thought they were chrysanthemums."

She acted as if he'd defamed her family and besmirched her name. "Those are lilies, sir." Her flat New England accent seemed to grow broader with every word.

He was beginning to remember just how much he hated Boston.

"Look, I don't care if they're called Volkswagens," he said, jet lag destroying his normal good humor. "This is the effect I want. If you can't do it, I'll go somewhere else."

For twenty-five minutes he'd been trying to duplicate the incredible fire flowers he and Katie had enjoyed in Hakone. Such flights of romantic fancy were obviously foreign to the Pilgrim on the other side of the counter.

Yankee thrift, however, came to his rescue. The thought of a sale walking out the door seemed to release the woman's imagination, and ten minutes later Tom had a pretty decent display of peonies, chrysanthemums, lilies and carnations.

After the air-conditioned store, the sidewalks seemed more sweltering than before. He started on his way to Katie's home in Beacon Hill. His feet stuck to the asphalt as he crossed the street.

The usual lunch-hour rush had slowed to a lazy crawl as sweat-soaked pedestrians sought shelter in restaurants and stores.

Beacon Hill was on the other side of the Boston Common, and he cut through the park to save time. Businessmen and women sprawled under the shade trees, sipping sodas. Kids played in the pond. Lovers necked openly, too besotted to give propriety a second thought.

All in all, it was a beautiful, pastoral sight in the middle of the big city bustle, but it did nothing for him.

He still hated Boston as much as he had when he'd been at Harvard. The city limits chafed against him. Concrete and steel boundaries fenced in his soul until he found it hard to breathe. His gaze bounced off glass and granite instead of open land and infinite sky.

It reminded him of other times, of people who no longer existed—except in his memory.

When Paula accepted a scholarship at Radcliffe, Buck Sagan had decided—with the Westerner's usual insecurity—that an Eastern education was just what his high-spirited, irresponsible son needed.

So Tom, whose intellectual curiosity back then had been barely measurable, was packed off to Harvard to become civilized.

Paula excelled.

Tom failed with flying colors.

In the middle of his sophomore year, he'd packed all of his belongings in the back of a '63 Ford Falcon station wagon that had seen better days and headed for Las Vegas and home.

He got there fifteen months later.

The beauty of the country, the lure of no deadlines, no schedules, no pressure, had been more than the nineteen-year-old boy could resist. He worked his way from Boston down to Florida and back up, then finally headed across the vast plains of the Midwest toward home.

Buck had been waiting for him with an ultimatum: back to Harvard or into the navy. Two months later Tom was floating somewhere in the South China Sea. The prodigal son returned to Las Vegas when he was twenty-five, civilized but not tamed. He'd seen enough of the world to know that the deserts and canyons of his native Nevada were where he belonged. Freedom was a state of mind as well as a place, and he felt most free in the land he best understood.

And, although he fought against joining Sagan Fireworks, Inc., the pulls of family responsibility grew harder to ignore. He was as much a part of the company as he was part of the family; the two were indivisible.

When Buck and Paula died on that soft summer night, a part of Tom died with them.

Forty years of hard work and integrity fell into Tom's hands. Forty years of a man's life laid themselves across his shoulders. Paula's unfulfilled potential became a part of his wayward heart.

He no longer wondered what he was going to do with his life. Life, in no uncertain terms, had decided that for him.

Tom exited the Common and waited impatiently for a break in traffic so he could cross Beacon Street.

To hell with memories and responsibility and the old yoke of guilt he'd carried for so long now.

In a few days he'd be back in Las Vegas, caught up again in his obsession with the contest.

But for this wonderful moment out of time, he was going to pretend there was no one else on earth except himself and Katie Powers, the woman he'd traveled halfway around the world to see just one more time.

What he was doing was insane—the act of a desperate and deranged man whose heart was clearly in control of his brain.

She might slam the door in his face.

She might call the police.

She might not even recognize him away from the magic and splendor of that night on the mountainside.

He didn't care.

She had made him feel whole again; she had made him feel joyful when he'd thought joy a part of his past.

And if the dream faded in the face of reality—well, that was a chance he'd have to take.

He turned the corner onto Acorn Street.

He'd know soon enough.

Katie Powers was in a terrible mood that afternoon, and Nicole Travis was unfortunate enough to be in the line of fire.

"Damn it, Katie! You didn't have to snap my head off again." Nicole's dark brown eyes glared at her.

Katie looked up from her word processor and tried to rein in her temper.

"I didn't snap your head off, Nicole. I simply asked you if you'd done the artwork for the Weymouth job yet."

"It wasn't what you said so much as the way you said it." Nicole, a free-lance graphic artist, got up from the drafting table in the corner of Katie's enormous living room and stretched.

Katie had taken on a menu-planning and ad-design account for a downtown Boston restaurant, and for the past two days Nicole had been working at Katie's apartment to help meet an impending deadline. "I'll be kind and attribute your foul mood to jet lag."

Katie's response was less than kind.

"Are you *sure* you had a good time with your sister? You've been bitchy as hell since you got home last week."

Nicole was right. What Nicole didn't know, however, was that Katie's mood had been just as ugly before she left Japan. At the airport, Gwen had applauded the boarding announcement for Flight 411.

Katie's good nature had taken a dramatic turn for the worse after the night she had spent with Tom Sagan.

She glanced at the grandfather clock in the hallway. "Why don't we break for lunch?"

Nicole brightened. "Want to race around the corner for some Chinese?"

"You go. I'm going to take a nap." Sleep certainly couldn't make her disposition any worse.

"So it's jet lag, after all. I was beginning to worry, Katie. You've been tense as hell."

"No need to worry." Katie stood up. "I just never expected to come home to such a load of work. I'm going to have to reorganize my schedule."

"You have some great prospects," Nicole said, grabbing her purse from the closet. "If it keeps going like this, you'll have to open a real office with a water-cooler and everything."

Katie groaned. "Go to lunch. All I want to do right now is close my eyes and sleep."

"I'll bring you back some hot-and-sour soup," Nicole said as Katie unlocked the massive mahogany door that opened onto the quiet, tree-lined street. "It does wonders for jet lag."

"What is that—the yuppie equivalent of chicken soup?"

Nicole was still laughing as she jogged off down the street.

Amazing. How anyone could jog in such oppressively hot and humid weather was beyond Katie. Boston had been blanketed with a heat wave since she had returned from Japan, and Katie had spent most of her time tucked away in her renovated town house with its blessed central air-conditioning.

Historic preservation was wonderful, but she'd bet even Abigail Adams would have sold the farm for a decent night's sleep during a Boston summer.

At that particular moment, central air-conditioning seemed to be the only thing in her life that Katie was still satisfied with.

Certainly nothing else seemed to suit her anymore.

From the second she had arrived home from her trip to Japan, Katie felt as if someone had sneaked into her Boston life while she was on vacation and jumbled things up just enough that she couldn't quite get her bearings.

Her narrow four-story house seemed cavernous. Her fancy sports car seemed about as exciting as a 1956 DeSoto. Her elegant clothes could be given to the Salvation Army and replaced with jeans and T-shirts for all it mattered.

Even the quiet, peaceful life-style she'd cultivated seemed fashioned for another woman. She couldn't figure out where she'd once fitted into the scheme of things.

Sleep had to help.

She kicked off her sandals and stretched out on her bed, not even bothering to turn down the antique patchwork quilt or slip out of her shorts and T-shirt. She closed her eyes.

Nothing.

Her heart pounded as if she were in caffeine overdrive. Her mind bounced restlessly from thought to thought, somehow always circling back around Tom Sagan and the feel of his lips on hers.

She could get up and do some more work. God knew, she had a thousand calls to return—including three from Bob about the job offer at Bernstein, Jameson and Coulter—but no energy to return them.

And no interest, either.

If she were anything but the logical, practical woman she was, she'd toss this whole mess over and start fresh. Maybe in Chicago.

Or Houston.

She thought of Tom's beautiful eyes.

Or Las Vegas.

"Good going, Powers," she mumbled into her pillow. "A mid-life crisis at twenty-eight."

Stepping out of character was dangerous for an orderly person. It was much, much better to keep to the main road and ignore those tantalizing little side paths, no matter how seductive those side paths might be.

No matter how tall or how blond or how—

Saved by the bell.

The melodic eight tones of the Westminster chimes cut her fantasy off at the pass. When May-Chan's Szechuan Palace had decided to enter the fast-food field Katie had no idea, but she would have to remember to thank the chef next time she saw him. She raced to the front door.

"I hope you brought the hot-and-sour soup anyway, because I—"

"I would have if you'd told me, Katie. Will flowers do instead?"

There on her doorstep stood Tom Sagan, carrying the biggest bouquet of peonies and chrysanthemums she'd ever seen.

She was staring up at him with those enormous blue eyes of hers, and he started to wonder if he'd made one hell of a mistake. Sweat beaded on his brow and it had nothing to do with the temperature.

"Well, Katie Powers, are you going to invite me in, or do I leave my flowers on the doorstep and make a dignified retreat?"

"You can't be here. You're in Japan."

Tom bent forward and kissed her lightly on the mouth. "I'm here, Katie. In the flesh."

It was her flesh, however, that occupied his mind.

He looked down at her legs, long and bare in white shorts, and took careful note of the glorious line of thigh and calf he'd only wondered about before. Her feet were bare, her toenails polished a dusty pink. Her wavy red hair rose up and around her face like living fire, and no matter how you looked at it, she was infinitely more beautiful than he'd remembered.

She was still staring at him as if she expected him to grow horns and a tail when a horrible thought popped into his head.

"I'm, uh, I'm not interrupting anything, am I?"

Her sister, Gwen, hadn't mentioned anything about there being a man in Katie Powers's life, but big sisters—especially ones who were several thousand miles away—didn't know everything. If a man suddenly appeared at her side, he'd mutter something about FTD florists and stumble back down the steps with whatever dignity he could manage.

Finally, she seemed to surface from the fog she'd been in. "I'm in shock," she said. "I have no idea how on earth you managed to find me."

"If you invite me in, I'll tell you. I'm too jet-lagged to be dangerous." *Subtle, Tom, real subtle.*

"Of course you can come in," she said, her voice just a tad testy, "but you'd have gotten a better welcome if I'd been prepared."

He stepped into the cool, dark hallway and waited while she locked the door behind him.

"Your sister didn't tell you that I came by her apartment the day after you left?"

She led him up a narrow staircase to a bright and airy kitchen on the second floor.

"No, she didn't." She pulled an enormous white vase out of a high cupboard. The right side of her turquoise T-shirt rose with her movement, exposing a tanned and trim waist. "How on earth did you know where my sister lives?"

He handed her the massive bouquet of flowers. "She gave me her address and phone number the night you shoved the phone in my chest."

She looked at him over the bright pink cloud of peonies. "I didn't shove the phone in your chest."

"I have the bruises to prove it."

"So, that's it—you're suing me for damages. Is there a subpoena hidden in the chrysanthemums?"

"Only if I have to subpoena you to have dinner with me tonight."

She turned on the faucet to fill the vase with water. "Did Gwen put you up to this?"

"The subpoena or the dinner?"

"Either one."

"That's a pretty elaborate practical joke, wouldn't you say?"

"I wouldn't put anything past my sister."

Her head was bent over the vase as she arranged the shocking-pink peonies and the multicolored chrysanthemums. He noticed that her hands trembled slightly. It hadn't occurred to him that this might be as difficult for her as it was for him.

"Look at me, Katie." He stepped closer to her.

That touch of sadness he'd noticed before was in her lovely eyes once more.

"You're a fantasy, Tom," she said softly. "Fantasies have no business showing up on my doorstep."

"Not even if they come bearing gifts?"

"Not even then. Don't you know fantasies can't survive the real world?"

Some did. At the moment, he was banking on that assumption.

"I tried to find you again," he said, moving still closer. The haunting, familiar scent of her perfume made him dizzy. "You told me you'd be in Tokyo through the twentieth."

"The difference in time zones confused me. I left on the nineteenth."

"So I found out."

"This is insane," she said, her voice soft. "Why are you here?"

Because something inside me switched back to life when I first saw you. Because I have to find out if this is more than fantasy.

He had less than a month to master Ogatsu's secrets or to discover the illusory blue of an emerald's fire. Back home the work was going on without him as it had so many times before.

He had no business being in Boston, no business courting Katie Powers, whose secrets and insecurities would only complicate his life. He belonged back in Las Vegas at the compound with everyone else, not jet-lagged and out of control in the very proper kitchen of a very proper Boston businesswoman.

"Damned if I know, Katie," he said finally, pulling her into his arms. "Damned if I know."

Until that moment, Katie had believed the magic had been a part of the evening on that faraway mountainside, a part of the ancient festival, something rare and fleeting and as dependent upon circumstance as upon chemistry.

She was wrong. Dead wrong.

Pressed back against her Formica counter with its cold edge hard against her thigh, she found herself as enchanted, as mesmerized, as she had been on that night of fireworks and ancient splendor.

Her own prosaic kitchen could contain magic.

How wonderful.

How dangerous.

His tongue lightly traced the contour of her lower lip, and she sighed and allowed him entry.

How delicious.

Her body's hard angles softened, melting against his power with a voluptuous grace unknown to her before. *Stop while you still can,* a tiny voice warned. Madness sometimes presented itself in the most tempting of packages.

"Tom." She broke the kiss and placed her hand on his chest. The thudding of his heart beneath her palm was a potent aphrodisiac. "This isn't the way I normally spend my lunch hour."

He nipped the side of her neck gently and she shivered with delight. Much too exciting. She moved away and pretended to fuss with the flowers.

"Nicole will be back any moment with—"

"Hot-and-sour soup?"

"Hot-and-sour soup."

"Is Nicole another sister?"

"Business associate."

"Can't you tell her to take the rest of the day off?"

"Not with a deadline twenty-four hours away."

"Bad timing?"

"Let's just say less than perfect."

"I should have called."

She couldn't read the expression on his face. His beautiful golden eyes betrayed nothing. "Why didn't you?"

"Because I had to see you, Katie. I had to prove to myself that you were real, that I hadn't imagined you."

They were words she'd longed to hear in the heart of the night, a lover's words holding her fast with promise. The private, secret litany of a woman of reason, behind whose facade hid the soul of a romantic heroine.

"I don't know what to say, Tom."

"Say you'll have dinner with me."

She hesitated.

He touched her hair. "I've come a long way to break bread with you, Katie Powers."

"I have other obligations."

"I understand that."

"I don't think you do, Tom. Perhaps you have more flexibility than I do. Maybe another—"

"There is no other time, Katie. I'll be here until Sunday, then I have to go back to Vegas."

"You're very persistent." She'd never been pursued before and didn't know how to act.

"I know that." His hand wound around her hair, gently pulling her back into his arms. "Persistence is one of my virtues."

"And you're not terribly subtle." They were so close that his scent filled her mind with imagined delights.

"We don't have time for subtlety."

"This is crazy," she murmured as he kissed her throat and shoulders. "This is no more real than what we shared in Japan."

"If this isn't real, we'll find out soon enough," he said, his breath warm and moist now against her lips. His hands cupped her breasts and she shuddered with pleasured shock.

She was having trouble forming a coherent sentence. "There's no future to this relationship."

"Maybe not."

"We barely know each other."

"We have four days to learn."

"We probably have nothing in common."

"We'll find out soon enough, won't we?"

"I suppose you have an answer for everything."

He moved away from her slightly so she could look into his eyes. "No, Katie. I don't have any answer at all for the way you've made me feel."

Anticipation, dark and thrilling, rose inside her chest. "I'm not an impulsive woman, Tom."

"So I've noticed."

"I don't believe in love at first sight, or in thunderbolts or Cupid's arrow."

"Poor Katie with the logical heart."

Poor Katie's heart felt anything but logical as it beat double time inside her chest.

"Give us a chance, Katie. Let's see what this is all about."

"It's not every day a man flies halfway around the world to have dinner with me," she said, feeling a crazy grin slide over her face. "The least I can do is cook it for him."

Tom's handsome face became incandescent with an expression so openly vulnerable, so intimate, that Katie had to look down at the bright pink peonies and multicolored mums to regain her composure.

What kind of charmed life had this man lived that he could express joy so simply, so without fear?

"I'm staying at the Westin," he said and gave her the room number. "You name the time and I'll bring wine and dessert."

"Eight o'clock, and if you can find some cannoli, I'll break out my best champagne for the occasion."

"Your wish is my command." He stifled a yawn. "Sorry, Katie. I'm still on Tokyo time."

She walked him back down to the front door. "Get some sleep," she said. "I want you wide awake and hungry enough to enjoy my lasagna."

"I may be a little drowsy, but there's one thing I can guarantee you, Katie Powers: I'll be hungry."

There was no mistaking his meaning. Katie never knew it was possible to blush from head to foot.

Obviously, she still had a lot to learn.

Tom winced and held the telephone receiver away from his ear. "Keep talking, Molly. If you get any louder, we won't need AT&T."

"We don't use AT&T," she shot back. "We use Sprint, and don't change the subject. I want to know why you're not in Japan."

"Watch it, little sister. I'm still your boss."

Molly's inventive use of language never failed to amaze him. " . . . sideways," she finished.

"Better check out your copy of *Gray's Anatomy*," he said, bunching up the bed pillow beneath his neck. "I don't think it's possible."

Molly ignored him. "You were supposed to get home this morning. What happened?"

"Would you believe I forgot?"

"Try telling that to Ed and the rest of the crew. Better come up with a better one than that."

"I ran into a snag."

Molly groaned. "Don't tell me you didn't accomplish anything over there, because I—"

"Cool down, Molly," he broke in. "I just spent two days with Umeki in Kyoto and came away with more information than I ever expected."

"Then why aren't you back here? Eddie's acting like a slave driver, Bobby forgot to ground himself on the copper plate outside Building C last Friday and scared hell out of Carlos, and Mother's driving everyone crazy with her time-and-motion studies."

"Business as usual. They probably don't even know I'm gone."

"Well, I can't stand it anymore," Molly said. "I'm not a good administrator." She paused. "I don't have the slave driver instinct."

His laugh bounced off the walls of his hotel room. "You could have fooled me."

"I'm serious, Tom. You're the one obsessed with winning this contest. You're the one who should be here holding down the fort."

Right on target as usual. Time to change the subject. "Have you been working on the sketches for the finale?" Molly was an artist whose works had appeared in a number of prestigious galleries in the Southwest.

"I don't have time, Tom. In case you don't remember, you left me in charge, and this place has been crazier than the Golden Nugget on a Friday night."

"Don't worry. I swear I'll be home Sunday night."

"Do you mind telling me where you're calling from, if you're not in Japan?"

"I'm in Boston."

"Boston!" He winced again as her voice climbed another two decibels. Pretty soon only dogs would be able to hear her. "You hate Boston."

"I know."

"So what are you doing there?"

"Unfinished business."

"Do you have a sudden yen to finish your education?"

"Mind your own business, Molly."

"Your business *is* my business, brother dear. We all own a part of Sagan Fireworks."

He started to say he was in Boston on a personal matter, but the thought of being subjected to another round of Molly's ceaseless questions was daunting in the extreme.

"We'll talk about it on Sunday."

"This doesn't make any sense, Tom. First you go halfway around the world to spy on the competition, then you casually stop over in a city you hate for a four-day vacation." Her voice actually softened with concern. "I'm worried about you."

"Worry about getting two thousand shells completed by the time I get back."

"Damn that stupid competition. I'm sick of hearing about it. You can win every contest there is and it's still not going to bring Daddy and Paula back. I mean winning is good for business, but—"

It was an old argument and he stopped listening while she ranted.

Molly, probably the world's only practical artist, didn't understand symbolism or the unspoken debt a man can owe both his father and the woman he once loved.

To Molly, Sagan Fireworks was strictly business, and a world-class contest just a way to garner publicity.

And why not? She wasn't the one who'd failed. He was.

"You're a philistine, Mol," he said, cutting her off at last. "There's no hope for you."

"And you're a pigheaded, romantic fool. Stop chasing after shooting stars and get back here where you belong. If this damned contest is so important, what in hell are you doing in Boston?"

"Chasing after shooting stars."

"So help me, Thomas Allard Sagan, when I get my hands on you, I'll—"

"See you Sunday, Molly."

Click.

He folded his arms behind his head and looked up at the ceiling. Waves of exhaustion made the bed feel like a small boat rocking in a storm-tossed sea. He was so jet-lagged that not even Molly's amateur psychoanalysis got under his skin.

He set his travel alarm and closed his eyes.

Images of Katie Powers trailing long, glittering robes of gold and silver fire in the night sky over Hakone lured him into a deep and dream-filled sleep.

"Tomorrow morning should do it." Katie pushed her chair back from her Kay-Pro and stood up. "If you can finish up the layout at home tonight, Nicole, you can call it a day."

Nicole, hunched over the drafting table, made no motion to leave. Katie glanced at the clock. Five-fifteen. She had promised Tom dinner at eight.

"Nicole! Quitting time."

"Give me another hour," Nicole mumbled. "I'm almost done."

"Any other time," Katie said, "but not tonight."

Nicole looked up. "Jet lag?"

Katie, who should have known better, shook her head no. "I'm having someone over for dinner."

"Male or female?"

"Male."

Nicole had her portfolio closed and her bag packed in record time.

"I was wondering why you were whistling while you worked," she said as Katie unlocked the front door for her. "I figured it was either a man or you had a Disney fetish."

Katie chuckled and opened the door. "Don't tell anyone, but I've always had a yen for Sneezy."

Nicole groaned as a blast of summer heat invaded the air-conditioned hallway. "Just keep your hands off Doc," she said as she started down the steps to the street. "Mother always wanted me to marry a professional man."

Katie hurried back upstairs to the kitchen. She breathed a prayer of thanks that she really did have lasagna in her freezer, and set about making a salad. A loaf of Italian bread rested on the counter. Champagne chilled in the refrigerator, an oddly elitist touch to a peasant meal, but it tickled her sense of the absurd.

She was just about to step into the shower when the telephone rang. She stared at it.

He's not coming. He's going back to Las Vegas tonight. He made a mistake. . . .

"Hello?"

"I was beginning to wonder if you were ever coming home, Kate." Robert Morrisson, her ex-husband.

"I've been home a week," she said, sitting down on the edge of the bed.

"Did you get my messages?"

"All three of them. I've been very busy."

"They really want you to join the firm, Kate. Old man Jameson is hot to get you doing the brochures for the year-end review."

"I haven't made up my mind yet, Bob."

"It's not because of me, is it?"

"Not at all." She and Bob had parted amicably. They were better friends now than during the last months of their marriage. "I may try it on my own."

"Free-lancing is risky business, Kate. Think of all you'll be giving up. B, J and C has the best pension plan in the Northeast."

I'm only twenty-eight, she thought. *Give me a break.* "I have until the end of the month to decide, haven't I?"

"Technically, yes, but your indecision is beginning to grate on Jameson's nerves."

"I'll just have to take my chances, I guess."

Silence. Then, "Did you have a good time with Gwen and Hiro?"

"Terrific."

"Any culture shock when you got there?"

"No," she said. "The culture shock came when I got home." Another long pause. This time she knew it was her turn. She took a deep breath and closed her eyes. "How are Sunny and the baby?"

"Fantastic. Sophie's gained almost a pound since we brought her home." All traces of the professional disappeared when he spoke about his new daughter.

The pain was greater than she'd remembered. It surprised Katie that it could feel so sharp, so new. "Obviously parenthood is agreeing with you."

His voice grew quieter. "Yes, it is."

Her throat ached with months of unshed tears. She swallowed hard. "Listen, Bob, I really have to go. I'm expecting a dinner guest and I have so much to do."

His professional voice was back in place. "I understand. Why don't we meet for lunch in the middle of next week and talk about your coming to work for us? Maybe a little in-person pep talk will sway you."

She smiled. "Maybe."

"Take care, Kate."

"Give my best to Sunny."

How strange, she thought as she replaced the receiver in the cradle. She had just spoken to the man she'd grown up with, the man she'd eaten with, made love to and slept beside for eight years of her life, and she felt no more connected to him than she did to the elevator operator in Gwen's apartment building in Tokyo.

Robert Morrisson had been a fixture in her life from fifth grade on, as much a part of her family as her parents or her sister, Gwen. She liked him, admired him, enjoyed his subtle wit and keen intelligence. Both families had declared them a "match made in heaven" and it seemed foolish to disagree.

No two people were more suited to each other temperamentally than Katie and Bob. They liked peace and quiet and order; they believed in IRAs, money market accounts and balanced checkbooks.

Gwen used to tease them mercilessly about their penchant for planning life down to the last detail.

"I bet you two even have a timetable for conception hanging over the bed," Gwen had said, making her own straitlaced husband, Hiro Mifune, look as uncomfortable as Katie felt.

Gwen, of course, wasn't far from wrong.

When Katie announced her pregnancy on the evening of her twenty-fifth birthday, Katie and Bob were right on schedule.

When Jill was born on a cool Sunday morning in April, everyone remarked on the efficiency and ease of the birth. Katie and Bob made room in their lives for their daughter with the practiced skill of longtime parents.

However, when Jill died in her crib sometime in the middle of a sultry June night, Katie and Bob fell apart. Two intelligent, relentlessly logical adults—and neither one was capable of reaching out in sorrow to comfort and hold.

They tried marriage counseling and marriage encounters, a Caribbean cruise and a trial separation, but still they were unable to overcome the pain of this ultimate failure.

The nursery was now a study with an enormous rolltop desk of the same lustrous pine that Jill's cradle had been. If she looked closely on a sunny morning, the faint ghosts of Disney murals showed through the delicate Laura Ashley wallpaper Robert had put up after the baby's death.

Soon after the divorce, Bob had married Sunny, a woman whose personality actually suited her name. Sunny owned an offbeat boutique in the marketplace at Faneuil Hall and the sight of Bob in his ubiquitous three-piece suit standing next to this woman with the punked hair and outrageous leather skirts invariably caused heads to turn. Anyone could see that Bob and Sunny were the most ridiculous match on earth.

Anyone could see that Bob and Sunny were also ridiculously happy.

But for Katie, the fact that out of this unlikely union had come an infant daughter named Sophie was the most amazing fact of all.

Katie stood up and slipped out of her T-shirt and shorts and headed toward the bathroom.

Cautious Robert Morrisson, whose patterns of logic and emotion were so like her own, had taken a giant leap of faith and made it to the other side, while Katie peeked over the edge and saw how long a fall it would be.

She turned on the shower and stood under the spray.

None of it made sense, but then, perhaps none of it had to.

The fact that Tom Sagan, fireworks spy, had followed her all the way from Tokyo to Beacon Hill made no sense, either, but the fact remained that in a little over an hour, he would be at her doorstep for the second time that day, bearing wine and cannoli and expecting a lasagna dinner.

Tom Sagan wasn't part of her plan.

He was too carefree, too footloose, much too dangerous for a woman who needed security and structure.

But when she was near him, she felt as if one of those red-and-silver comets had gone off inside her heart and showered her with stars.

Maybe for the moment that was more than enough.

6

Tom hadn't been so nervous since he was fifteen years old and had stood at the front door of Linda Davis, the prettiest girl in his sophomore class.

Okay, so now he was a little taller, a little older and supposedly a hell of a lot more sophisticated, but as he stood at Katie Powers's front door in Beacon Hill carrying a box of cannoli from an Italian bakery in the North End and a bottle of Asti Cinzano, the nervous anticipation was just as bad as it had been at fifteen.

Ring the bell, Sagan. What the hell are you waiting for? Flying halfway around the world to show up unexpectedly had been easier than coming for dinner tonight. Grand gestures carried with them their own excitement. This evening that he'd all but forced Katie into had to create its own magic.

This time they couldn't rely on fireworks or moonlight or surprise.

They were on their own.

Katie peeked out the living room window for the fourth time. Tom Sagan was still standing on her narrow stoop in the same place he'd been standing for the past five minutes.

What on earth was the matter with him?

She'd been straightening the pillows on her sofa and trying to ignore the way her stomach kept doing double flips when she saw Tom get out of a cab in front of her house. She raced to the hall mirror to check her makeup, to smooth down her hair—which had become wildly wavy, thanks to the humidity—and to adjust the belt on her turquoise jumpsuit.

The lasagna was ready to pop into the microwave. The salad was prepared. Champagne chilled in the refrigerator.

She was as ready as she'd ever be.

The only trouble was, Tom hadn't gotten around to ringing the doorbell yet.

Being a few minutes late was one thing: Even a chronic clock-watcher like Katie managed to allow fifteen minutes' slack in a dinner invitation. And, God knew, carefree Tom Sagan didn't seem the type of man who paid much heed to punctuality. But to arrive on time only to stand on her doorstep twiddling his thumbs—that was enough to make her crazy.

"Will you ring the bell, damn it?" she said out loud.

At seven minutes after eight her patience finally eroded and she marched downstairs to the front door, unbolted it and opened it wide.

He was leaning against the railing, looking splendidly sexy in cream-colored pants and a dark gold polo shirt.

"Just answer this question and you can sit out here as long as you like," she said as he stared at her in surprise. "Are you ever going to ring this damned bell?"

"Yes. I'm trying to be fashionably late."

She wanted to tell him no one in Boston was fashionably late, but she held her tongue. "What time do you plan on ringing it?"

He looked at his watch. "In one minute and thirty seconds."

"Fine."

She closed the door and counted down.

"...four...three...two...one—"

Right on cue, the chimes began to toll.

She opened the door again. He stood ramrod straight in front of it, a box of cannoli from DeVito's in one hand and a bottle of Asti Cinzano in the other. His smile was as devastating as she remembered.

"Come in," she said. "You're right on time."

He followed her up the stairs to the kitchen. "No, I'm not. I'm ten minutes late."

"You said that was fashionable."

He put the sparkling wine and the pastries down on the countertop.

"Somehow I don't think you agree." The twinkle in his eye told her he was enjoying this encounter as much as she was.

"I saw your cab pull up at seven fifty-nine. You've been standing on my step for eleven minutes."

"Did you have a stopwatch on me?"

"I can't help it. Digital clocks make precision unavoidable."

"Don't tell me you're one of those Type A personalities who sleep with their watches on."

"Okay, I won't," she said. "I keep it on my night table."

"Must do wonders for your sex life."

"I've had no complaints." Of course she'd had no complaints; at the moment, she had no sex life to speak of.

Katie put the Asti in the refrigerator and took out the Moët. She didn't dare turn around because she was certain the expression on her face would give her away.

"I hate watches," Tom said as she led him up another flight of stairs to the living room. "That's the first thing to go when I'm on vacation."

She glanced over her shoulder and saw a bulky Seiko chronograph on his left wrist. "You're wearing one now."

"When a punctuality freak invites you for dinner, it's a necessity."

"How did you know I was a punctuality freak?" As far as she could remember, this topic had never come up before.

"When I meet a woman who has a Rolex on her wrist, a Timex in her pocketbook and a train schedule on her lap, I'll give you even money she could tell you the exact time in three languages."

"Four languages," she said as they approached the third-floor landing, "including Latin and Serbo-Croatian."

"And I'll bet you know how to say, 'You're late,' in every one of them."

"Guilty." She laughed as he leaned against the wall and pretended to gasp for breath after the long climb. "It's a curse passed down from my father. He said I was born with a stopwatch in my hand."

"I'll bet you were early."

"Two weeks." Katie motioned him toward the sofa in the center of the living room. "They were still on the Cape at the summer house. My father had to break all the speed limits from Hyannis to Boston to get Mother to the hospital in time.''

He sank down into the overstuffed sofa and stretched his long legs out in front of him. The sight of his running shoes against her elegant parquet floor was as charming as it was incongruous.

''You would have saved your folks a lot of trouble if you'd been fashionably late.''

''I think we've come a full circle, Tom.'' She put the bottle of Moët on top of the oak bar near the window and pulled down two hollow-stemmed flutes. ''You still haven't told me why you stood outside on my doorstep for eleven minutes.''

''Would you believe I had a bad case of the jitters?''

She laughed out loud. ''I'd believe I had a bad case of jitters, but you? Try again.''

His high-wattage smile faded. ''I'm not teasing you, Katie. It was tougher to ring that doorbell tonight than to show up unexpected this afternoon.''

Katie eased the cork out of the champagne bottle and poured the golden wine into the glasses. ''Very illogical,'' she pointed out as she handed him a glass. ''You had an invitation tonight. This afternoon you didn't.'' She sat down on the chair opposite the couch.

''Exactly. If it didn't work out this afternoon, I could always blame it on being a pushy S.O.B.'' He broke eye contact for a split second. ''If it doesn't work out tonight...'' He shrugged and let his words die off.

''We could still blame it on your being a pushy S.O.B. I wouldn't mind.''

He gave her a sharp look. ''Thanks a lot, Powers. First dates are bad enough without adding verbal abuse.''

She raised her glass toward him. ''To first dates.''

He raised his glass. "To the Japanese Railway."

"To the end of fashionable lateness."

He leaned closer. "To Fate in all its infinite wisdom."

The way he was looking at her made Katie's knees knock.

He rose and stood so close that the heat from his body made her sway toward its source. She leaned farther backward.

"To getting dinner ready on time." She clicked her glass against his and stood up.

"To hell with dinner." He took her glass and put it down on the table with his.

Katie's breath caught as he turned back to her and looked into her eyes.

"I promised you lasagna," she said, wondering how much higher the tension between them could build. "I'm a woman of my word."

"I didn't come here only for lasagna."

His hands were at her waist, the tips of his thumbs at the bottom of her rib cage.

"I didn't think so."

You can stop this now, if you want to, Katie told herself. *All you have to do is smile and turn away.*

But she did neither. Something wild and hidden broke free inside her and she lifted her head up for his kiss, the kiss that had been between them since he showed up at her doorstep one minute early, yet fashionably late.

Her lips parted beneath his, and she could taste the exquisite fruity burst of champagne in her mouth as he deepened the kiss. Her hands traced the muscles of his biceps and trailed across the broad shoulders that strained against the confinement of his dark gold shirt.

A sensation that could be described only as white-hot lust exploded in her belly.

Cool and logical Katie undid the top button on Tom's shirt and allowed herself the violent pleasure of his rough chest against the palms of her hands.

He broke the kiss and slid the loose jumpsuit over her shoulders, until the curve of her collarbone and slope of her breasts were exposed to his mouth and eyes. She couldn't think, couldn't speak, could only concentrate on the way his mouth felt pressed against her throat, the way his thick mustache set her skin on fire. His hand cupped her breast and a moan, low and urgent, escaped her lips.

"You know what I want, Katie," he said, drawing her body closer to his. "I want to pick you up in my arms and carry you to your bed, then lie with you until morning. I've wanted that since I first saw you on the train platform with the sun in your hair."

She burned hotter than the sun where he touched her. The feel of him, hard and ready, against her thigh made her want to throw caution aside and give in once, just once, to madness.

But there were consequences to madness—consequences both real and imagined—and she hesitated just long enough for the flames to recede.

"Katie?"

She blinked and looked up at him as if she had just roused from a deep sleep.

"What do you want, Katie?" he asked softly. "Tell me."

She rested her forehead against his chest. The thick blond hairs felt cool and soft against her skin. She wondered how they would have felt against her breasts.

"I'm sorry," she said after a moment. "Everything's happening too fast. I can't keep my balance."

Those incredible golden eyes of his were fastened to her face. She had the strangest sensation that he understood all she couldn't say.

"I'll catch you if you fall, Katie."

"I don't like to fall."

He straightened the top of her jumpsuit, and the touch of his hands made her question her own sanity.

"It's not that I don't want to," she said. "But—"

"Come on," he said, buttoning his shirt. "Let's have dinner."

She caught a glimpse of herself in the hall mirror as they headed toward the staircase.

Coward.

Denial did wonders for a man's appetite.

Tom demolished most of the lasagna, all of the Italian bread and Katie's salad as well as his own before he began to make a dent in his hunger.

The only thing that could have satisfied him was if he'd swept the food onto the floor and stretched Katie, naked and willing, on the pine trestle table to savor the delights of her luscious body.

All in all, lasagna was one lousy substitute.

She had been warm and responsive in his arms. The feel of her hands on his body had sent his self-control plummeting.

And yet some gut-level instinct told him that he needed more than he'd first been seeking, that when they finally came together, he wanted everything she had to give.

Even if it was only for a while.

* * *

Dinner was over.

Katie and Tom were sitting on the sofa in her living room, drinking brandy and arguing over the respective merits of Boston and Las Vegas.

What had started out as a teasing debate over the cultural benefits of the Boston Museum of Fine Arts versus Caesar's Palace had quickly degenerated into a no-holds-barred regional fight.

Katie, whose dates since her divorce had been limited to staid bankers, stodgy stockbrokers and sober attorneys like her ex-husband, was having the time of her life.

"I hate Boston," Tom said flatly for the second time. "We should give it back to the British and admit our mistake."

Katie practically leaped across the couch for his throat. "Two hundred years ago, they would have shot you for a statement like that."

"Two hundred years ago, my family was on the Russian steppes. We had enough to worry about."

"How can you hate Boston? You haven't even been here twenty-four hours."

"That's twenty-four hours longer than I want to be here."

She sat back on the arm of the sofa and took a sip of her drink. "Why don't I call a cab for Logan Airport? There's a midnight flight to Las Vegas you might be able to catch."

"If you'll take it with me, Katie Powers, I will."

She ignored the invitation, and he grinned.

"Just tell me how you can judge a city on the basis of seeing the inside of a hotel room and one woman's apartment."

"Easy. I've been here before. I hated it then and I hate it now."

"Just because we don't hang neon lights from 'Old Ironsides' and have topless tour guides at the Old North Church is no reason to hate Boston."

His easy laughter filled the room. "Does brandy always make you this pigheaded?"

"I'm pigheaded naturally." If anyone else had called her pigheaded, she would have been mortally wounded. For Tom, it seemed a normal observation. "Brandy just brings it to the surface more quickly. Now, give me one reason why you hate Boston."

"You have lousy pizza."

"We have great pizza."

"It's too damned crowded here."

"Only at rush hour."

"It's too hot, too noisy, too old. You have to push your way past the skyscrapers to find the stars."

"I only asked for one reason."

"Ask me why I'm here." He moved closer to Katie and her skin began to tingle with sensation.

She wanted to look away, but the intensity of his gaze trapped her. She slid back down onto the sofa cushion. "Why are you here?"

"Because this is where you are."

"Poor Tom," she murmured as he drew her into his arms. "Trapped in Boston against his will."

"A prisoner," he said, his mouth just inches from her own.

"A captive." She leaned closer to him.

"Just a slave to desire."

His lips met hers and an untimely laugh bubbled up.

"I'm sorry," she said. "It was the 'slave to desire' that got me."

"That's what I get for reading Jackie Collins on the plane. Does slave of passion sound any better?"

She shook her head. "Still makes me laugh."

He ran his hands across the tops of her breasts and her laughter died in her throat.

"Practical, punctual Katie Powers," he murmured, his lips pressed against the base of her throat. "Doesn't want to hear any pretty words. Doesn't want to know how she makes me feel. Doesn't want me to tell her that..."

At that second, Katie didn't care how she made him feel. All she knew was the way her body yearned toward him with a fierceness that terrified and entranced her. She pushed him slightly away.

"Softer than... What?" He looked up at her, his beautiful golden eyes glittering with desire.

"Shut up, Tom."

Before she could think, before she could come up with a reason why this should never be, Katie put her arms around his neck and allowed logic to fall by the wayside, and desire, pure and wild, to take its place.

He felt wonderful beneath her hands. The strong muscles of his shoulders, the silky dark blond curls beneath her fingers, the heat of passion against her skin—all gathered forces to ignite a fire deep inside, a fire that leaped and crackled and threatened to rage out of control.

The feel of his tongue as it traced the outline of her lips conjured up images so erotic, so enticing, that her breathing quickened to keep pace with the crazy pounding of her heart.

She groaned with pleasure as he pressed her back against the cushioned arm of the sofa, fitting his length against her own, inviting her to draw closer to the source of his heat.

He traced the contours of her shoulders with his hands, then slid them slowly—agonizingly slowly—to her breasts. Through the silky fabric of her jumpsuit, her nipples tightened as his hands cupped her for a moment. The soft hiss of the zipper as he eased it down echoed in her brain.

"You're beautiful, Katie," he said as the jumpsuit slid from her shoulders, revealing her breasts and her obvious need for him. "I knew you would be beautiful."

But of course it was he who was beautiful. Just the sight of him leaning over her, more golden and glorious than a mere mortal had any right to be, was enough to send her spinning off into infinity.

The fact that he found her beautiful, that his body was responding to her nearness, was further proof of the strange and wonderful magic that had started on the other side of the world.

He bent his head to her breasts, and she arched up against him as he took one nipple deeply into his mouth. An answering tension began to build deep inside her loins, a pulsing, throbbing emptiness that only he could ease.

She wanted him more than she'd wanted anything in her life.

She didn't care if it was only for the moment. She didn't care if tomorrow morning she might regret what she'd done. All she cared about was giving in to the delicious madness that had driven reason from her mind and brought wild abandon to her soul.

She felt totally, gloriously, wonderfully alive.

He was beyond hunger.

The sight of Katie, half naked and more lushly beautiful than he'd imagined in his most secret fantasies, aroused a primitive need to possess, to devour. She fumbled with the waistband of his pants, and he helped her undo the button. The feel of her hand, warm and soft against him, brought him quickly to the brink.

"Not now, Katie," he murmured against her ear. "I want more time to show you how you make me feel."

She moved restlessly against him. There was a sense of wonder in her abandonment; it was visible in the unguarded glow in her cobalt-blue eyes, an uncensored joy he hadn't seen before. He wondered what had happened in her life to extinguish the fire that burned in her now.

His hand slid over her taut midriff, relishing the way her flesh quivered as he trailed a finger down as far as the silky jumpsuit would allow. The couch was narrow and their position awkward. They needed a bed, wide and welcoming, for all he wanted to do for her.

He moved away from her magical hands and stood up, not even trying to hide his obvious desire for her. He kicked off his shoes. She sat up, the sides of her jumpsuit barely covering her breasts. Her hair tumbled over her tanned shoulders in a wild tangle of waves. The melding of powerful sensuality and classic beauty was almost his undoing.

He slid down the zipper on his pants and hesitated. Those limitless eyes of hers never looked away.

There was no coyness, no subterfuge.

The act of baring himself before her gaze took on new implications. Before, he had wanted to please her with his caresses, with mastery and control and love. He'd wanted to make love to her from the first second he'd spotted her on the train platform in Japan a lifetime ago.

Now he wanted to do more.

Women before Katie had responded to his looks. He took for granted the glances on the street, the comments and whispers that followed him. Flattering, yes, but basically of no concern.

Until now.

He wanted the sight of his body, hot and hard and demanding, to make her cry out with desire. He wanted the sight of him to drive her to the same edge of delirium he was clinging to.

In moments, the rest of his clothing was on the floor, and he faced her, unable to control his body's rampant response to her nearness.

Unwilling to hide what he wanted to give her, both body and soul.

Unprepared for the exultation he felt when she stood up and, without a word, led him upstairs to her bedroom at the end of the hall.

Katie hesitated at the doorway to her bedroom. An instant of fear—fear of her own violent, unbridled passion—made her pause. But then Tom swept her up into his arms and carried her toward the bed by the window, and she was willingly lost to reason.

In the yielding and limitless darkness of her room, each movement, each sound carried with it a fluid grace born of desire. Even the awkward movements inherent in removing her jumpsuit flowed one into another until she was naked against him, her mind sparking crazily from the electrifying feel of his muscled body covering hers.

The smell of him, the sound, the touch set her on fire from within. Her skin burned with it.

"Katie." The sound of her name on his lips made her shiver with pleasure. "Come to me, Katie."

She opened her mouth for his kiss, drawing his tongue inside, savoring taste and texture. Each movement he made drew an answering response from her deepest, most secret self, a surging of blood that flowed hot and fast.

He found her with his hand, and for a moment reality threatened to break the spell, but she refused to let the old thoughts, old inhibitions stand in the way of the delights before them.

He rolled them onto their sides, bodies still entwined, hands seeking and finding and pleasuring. Desire was hot and dark and liquid, and it demanded its due.

She drew her hands over his belly and down until she cupped him in her palms, and then began a movement so long and voluptuous that he cried out her name.

In an instant she was on her back and he was poised, and she could think of nothing but how it would feel to welcome him deep inside.

"I don't want to hurt you."

How could he, when her body yearned and flowered for him?

"You won't," she said, urging him forward. "Don't worry."

"Are you protected, Katie?"

The blunt question broke through her fog. "My God!" She struggled to sit up. "I used to use a . . ."

She heard an intake of breath and expected him to fling her across the room, then stalk out of her life forever. It was exactly what she deserved.

"Tom, I'm sorry. I didn't expect to—"

"Neither did I, beautiful Kate."

She tried to get out of bed, to get as far away from her embarrassment as possible.

"Come back to me," he said in the darkness.

"But—"

"Use you imagination, Katie." His mouth found hers in a fierce kiss. "I think we can still find ways to love each other."

The thought of facing another pregnancy, another loss, terrified her. The fact that she had come so close to tempting fate was an indication of just how deeply attracted she was to this man.

She was totally vulnerable, with both her soul and her body exposed to him. Trusting him, an intimate stranger, was a dangerous leap into the unknown. But then his mouth moved lower and she discovered, to her intense delight, that he was indeed a man of his word.

He mentally recited the alphabet backward, the Preamble to the Declaration of Independence and the lyrics to "Santa Claus is Coming to Town" in an attempt to keep from giving in to the desire that built inside him.

Even in the darkness, he knew she was beautiful, that everything about her drove him mad with need. The dreams he'd had these past nights were nothing compared to the reality. The act of pleasuring her brought him closer to ecstasy than a hundred nights in another woman's arms.

And when she shuddered against him, her soft cries filling his head, he felt more powerful, more primitively male, more in danger of losing his heart than ever before.

He'd set out as the hunter and instead been captured by the game.

His surrender was swift and sweet.

Katie was glad the room was dark, for in daylight she could never have behaved with such delicious abandon. Tom Sagan lit up the room with shooting stars and soaring comets, taking her far beyond reality's reach.

She'd soared to the heavens faster, more smoothly, than ever before, and had discovered levels of passion—and ways of expressing it—mortal women couldn't guess at.

Now they lay together beneath her colonial patchwork quilt, listening to the sounds of the night street below her window.

"What's wrong with this picture?" She sounded embarrassingly sated and lazy.

He pulled her closer to him. "Absolutely nothing."

"Look closer," she said. "There's one minor imperfection."

His chuckle rumbled beneath her ear. "Turn on the lights and I'll look around."

"And bare my thighs to your critical eye? No, thanks."

His large hand slid down her supple flank. "A loving eye," he said, kissing her shoulder. "Never critical."

"The cannoli are downstairs," she said, thinking about the wonderful pastries filled with ricotta cheese and sugar and chocolate bits. "We should be feasting on pastry and champagne."

"How many flights down is the kitchen?"

"Three."

"I can live without it."

"I'm used to the stairs," she said, sliding toward the edge of the bed. "I'll be back in a flash."

"Are you implying I'm not in good enough shape to do it?" His masculine feathers had obviously been ruffled.

"Well, I did see you gasping for breath on the landing..." She let her words trail off innocently.

"I say I could get to the kitchen and back before you count to one hundred."

"I say you'll need CPR."

"I run three miles a day."

"I run six," she countered, "and those stairs sometimes do me in."

"Is that a challenge?"

"Yes."

He pulled her back across the bed, pinning her to the mattress with the wonderful weight of his muscular body. "And if I win the challenge?"

His mustache tickled her breasts and she laughed. "You get to eat all the cannoli."

"Not good enough."

A slow, lazy fire began to build inside her. "You get to drink half of the champagne."

"I need more motivation."

She stroked him lightly. "We'll think of something."

Tom was back upstairs with the pastries and champagne in nothing flat.

He wasn't even breathing hard.

" ... seventy-eight ... seventy-nine ..."

He turned on the overhead light. "Stop counting, Katie Powers. You lost the bet."

He had a glimpse of tantalizing peach-colored flesh just before she dived under the covers with the speed of a Cruise missile.

"Will you turn that damned light off, Tom?" she called from under the quilt. "No one over eighteen should be seen in direct light without her clothes on."

He put the tray down on the chest of drawers near the door. "You have nothing to be ashamed of, Katie."

"How do you know?" she mumbled. "The lights were off."

"I know by the way you feel."

"Turn the lights off, damn it."

"You can't stay there all night."

"Try me."

He already knew she was stubborn enough that she just might. He clicked the light off.

"My eyesight's twenty-twenty," he said, "but even with that, I can't pour champagne in the dark. Can we at least light a match?"

He heard her come out from under the quilt. What he wouldn't give to see her in the glorious altogether....

"The door to my study is at the other end of that wall," she said. "If you turn on the light in there, you'll be able to see."

"And you'll stay on top of the covers?"

God, how he loved the sound of her laugh. Amazing how quickly it was becoming part of his emotional memory.

"I promise."

He felt his way along the wall until he found the door to the study, then clicked on the switch. Recessed lighting bathed the study with a soft glow.

"Great room," he said, eyeing the oversize pine desk by the window. "Where did you—" He stopped. Either he was going crazy or the faintest image of Disney's Cinderella and her Prince Charming peeked through the fussy Victorian wallpaper. "You'd better get a new handyman," he said as he turned back to the bedroom, laughing. "Disney and Country French are a pretty odd combination. The last owners must have had a child who—"

"No, they didn't have a child," she said, her voice flat. "I did."

7

Katie's words echoed throughout the room.

She wished she could snap her fingers and go back in time to an hour ago when they were still in each other's arms. The tray he'd brought upstairs rested on top of her dresser, the champagne a vivid reminder of the giddiness she'd been feeling.

"I didn't know you have a child." He walked toward her, but even the splendid sight of his strong body was not enough to conjure up the magic again.

"I don't." *Just say it, damn it.* "She's dead."

She swung her legs out of the bed and reached for the pale blue robe draped over the chair by the window.

A thousand expressions seemed to pass across his face, and he stopped a few feet away from where she stood near the bed. "I am so sorry, Katie."

She just nodded as pain, sharp and fierce, swooped down upon her. She turned away for a moment and slipped on her robe, trying to gather her emotions together and force them back into line.

He draped himself in a sheet and said, "I've got to go downstairs to get dressed."

"I'll make coffee," she said, relieved that she needn't make any explanations. The time for champagne was obviously past.

She picked up the tray.

"Katie."

"Yes?" *Don't ask me,* she thought. *Just let it rest.*

He was shirtless, clad only in his pants, his body as golden as his eyes. "If you—" He stopped abruptly, as if he picked up the tension coiling itself inside her chest. "Make the coffee strong," he said, with a slow smile. "Jet lag is beginning to get to me."

For a second the tension eased. "Tom?"

He looked at her.

"Thank you." She headed for the door.

It had never occurred to Tom that she might have had a child.

He'd dated a few single mothers in the past, and usually the topic of their children entered into conversation early on. He'd taken Katie's silence on the subject to mean her marriage had been childless.

As obscene and unnecessary as the death of Paula and his father had been, the death of a child was more so. In the normal order of life, the child outlives the parent, and the parent takes comfort from the fact that she is spared that ultimate loss.

Katie hadn't been spared. Her words, "Godspeed, Jill," came back to him, one of the memories of their night in Japan.

He went to turn off the light in the study that had once sheltered her hopes and dreams. The ghosts of Cinderella and the Fairy Godmother disappeared when he flicked the switch.

"Godspeed," he said.

* * *

The intimacy of sex paled before the greater intimacy of sharing her loss with Tom. Despite the fact that she would have loved to lay her sorrow in his lap and have him make it disappear, Katie was too well versed in the art of self-control to do so. Not even with Robert, the father of her child, the one person whose sorrow equaled hers, had she been able to let the tears flow and the true healing begin.

The evening with Tom never recovered its sense of magic and promise. Conversation over coffee was awkward and disjointed. They talked about the Red Sox and the Patriots, diamond cutting and Picasso's view of women, but never once did they touch on what had happened upstairs.

Finally, it was time for him to leave. She called for a cab to take him back to the Westin.

"He promised a taxi in ten minutes," she said, hanging up the phone, "but you'd better give them twenty."

Tom, who looked exhausted and jet-lagged, smiled. "Minuteman Cabs needs a refresher course in punctuality?"

She poured him some more coffee. "Desperately."

He thanked her and drank it down quickly. "I think we'd better talk about it, Katie."

A cold feeling spread through her chest. "No."

He touched the back of her hand, which rested on the arm of the sofa. "Call me old-fashioned, but I can't make love to a woman in more ways than I knew existed, then say good-night as if nothing happened." His smile was amused and slightly anxious.

Her relief was unbounded. "Call me old fashioned, too." Sex was infinitely easier to explore than sorrow.

"I don't know what you're thinking, Katie, but I want to."

She looked down at their hands. His were large and strong-looking, deeply tanned. He wore a heavy onyx-and-gold ring on his right ring finger. Her hands with their polished oval nails looked fragile by comparison.

"Talk to me, Katie," he said, his voice low and urgent. "We don't have much time left."

"I like rules," she said carefully, "and I don't know what the rules are to this game."

For once the twinkle was missing from his eyes. "This isn't a game, Katie."

"Of course it's a game. Things like this don't happen in real life." Men didn't follow her halfway around the world, and she certainly didn't invite those men into her home or, more specifically, into her bed.

"There is an explanation," he said. "We're falling in love."

"We haven't known each other long enough to fall in love."

"Throw your watch away, Katie. There's no timetable involved in falling in love."

"People need time to get to know each other; they need shared interest, a common background—"

"And sometimes it just happens, Katie." She wanted to look away, but the intensity of his gaze held her captive. "Sometimes in the space of one heartbeat, it happens."

"I don't believe in love at first sight." She wanted to believe that even if she couldn't control life, she could at least control her own heart.

"I do. It can happen."

She smiled. "Maybe back in the days of yore." That highly romantic notion of *coup de foudre*, or thunderbolt, was the stuff of Shakespeare's sonnets and Tchaikovsky's ballets.

He didn't smile back. "Maybe it's still possible today."

"Don't say it, Tom."

He stood up and drew her to her feet. "Maybe now."

"Don't romanticize things," she said softly as he held her. "I'm not fragile and I won't break. I understand what's happening between us."

"I don't think you do."

"We're like those fireworks we saw," she said. "What we have is fiery and beautiful and ultimately gone in an instant. I can deal with that." How she wished she could believe her brave words.

"I can't." The buzzer sounded and she moved to press the intercom. Tom pulled her back into his arms and kissed her with a passion that made her weak with longing. He glanced at the clock. It was one minute after midnight. "Just four more days, Katie Powers."

"I know," she said. "Just four more days until you go back to Vegas."

"No," he said, his mouth brushing against hers. "Just four more days to prove that you're in love with me."

Foolish man, she thought, as she walked him downstairs to the front door. *I already know that.*

But she also knew that after those four days were up, he would return to his life and she would continue with hers, and all that would remain would be sweet memories of her walk on the wilder shores of love.

The buzzer sounded again and she pressed the intercom.

"Minuteman Cabs."

"Give me three minutes," Tom said into the speaker.

A static-filled male voice laughed. "I'll give you three hours, Mister. The meter's running starting now."

"You'd better go," Katie said. "Fares are horrendous in Boston."

Tom ignored her. "Four days, Katie. That's all I'm asking of you."

"I have a deadline."

"What kind?"

She told him about the advertising promotion due by that afternoon.

"Then I'll settle for three and a half days."

"You're crazy."

He kissed her. "Maybe."

"You won't take no for an answer, will you?"

"I will if you want me to."

She hadn't expected to have the burden of decision placed quite so firmly on her shoulders. How did he manage to keep forcing her out from behind the defenses she'd spent the last few years constructing?

"I suppose I owe it to Boston to help change your mind about my hometown," she said.

"You could be a goodwill ambassador."

"I'll pick you up at two o'clock," she said as they walked downstairs to the front door.

He looked at his watch. "I have twelve-ten," he said. "Let's synchronize."

She showed her own two bare wrists. "Just be on time."

"You're a tough woman," he said. "I like that."

The tough woman felt the rest of her defenses crumble around her feet. She hoped that when the three and a half days were over, she'd be able to rebuild them.

As she watched his cab pull away, she wondered if she would even want to.

* * *

The red light on the telephone was blinking when Tom let himself into his hotel room. He called the switchboard for his messages.

"Three from a Molly Sagan O'Reilly," the operator said in her flat, New England voice. "The number is—"

"Thanks," he interrupted. "I know the number."

What in hell was Molly calling about now? He'd just spoken to her today—or was it yesterday? Jet lag and just plain fatigue made it hard for him to keep his days straight.

He was feeling guilty enough about his unscheduled stop in Boston. If she was going to berate him again, he'd just—

"You have reached the offices of Sagan Fireworks, Incorporated, of Las Vegas, Nevada. No one is in right now. At the beep, please leave your name, your company's name, and a phone number where you can be reached, and one of our representatives will get back to you. Have a good day." *Beep.*

He winced. "Remind me to get rid of that 'Have a good day,'" he said into the phone. "It's Tom. Pick up the damned phone, Molly, before I fall asleep. What the hell are you doing calling me three times? I just spoke to you—"

Molly picked up the telephone. "Stop screaming, Tom. You almost woke up the baby." They all had business lines in their homes as well as in the office. "Where've you been? I've been trying you all night."

"None of your business." He was not pleased by the intrusion of reality. "What's up?"

"Everything. H & H fell through on their part of the bargain. We have to find a source for two thousand mortar casings pronto, or we're out of the contest."

Damn. "Check the files," he said, trying to control his anger. "You can call Stoller Brothers or Jeff Kalter."

"I did, for your information. They can't help us."

He thought for a minute, feeling the tug of conflicting needs. "Try Layton and Marshall; they usually have good inventory. Otherwise, Crown is the best."

He heard the sound of a pencil scratching on paper, then, "Did you have a good time tonight?"

He kept quiet.

"Tom? I asked if you had a good time tonight."

"Terrific."

"Where'd you go?"

"A Red-Sox game." He said the first thing he could think of, praying that the team was actually at Fenway Park.

"Who won?"

"I left before the end."

"You're a terrible liar, brother dear."

"And you're a pain in the butt, little sister."

"I wish you weren't being so secretive about everything."

"I'm not being secretive. I just needed some time to myself."

"You were by yourself for three weeks in Japan," she pointed out.

"That was business."

"This isn't?"

He grinned at her persistence. "No, it isn't."

"Pleasure?"

Definitely. "Personal."

"What's her name?"

"Nancy Reagan."

Molly started to laugh. "How will you weather the scandal?"

"We're leaving for Honduras tomorrow morning."

"What will the President think?"

"Why do you think we're leaving for Honduras?"

"You're not going to tell me, are you?"

"Good thinking, Mol."

"Is she pretty?"

"I'll call you tomorrow to see what happens with the mortar casings. Good night, Mol."

Before Molly could ask one more question, he hung up the phone.

He couldn't blame Molly for being curious. His behavior at the moment was definitely out of character. For most of his thirty-two years he'd been as open as the land in which he was raised. This need for privacy was something brand-new.

He'd have a lot of explaining to do when he got back home Sunday night.

Sunday, however, was a long time from now.

For the next three and a half days, he was going to try to banish Molly and the competition and the guilt that still lingered, and concentrate solely on the beautiful Katie Powers.

The only fireworks he wanted to see were the ones they would create together.

After Tom left, Katie was too unnerved to sleep. She cleaned up the living room, did the dishes, straightened the kitchen, then started upstairs to the bedroom, only to find herself wide awake.

Each time she closed her eyes to sleep, her mind raced into double time, unleashing a crazy, distorted collage of faces and sounds that threw her into both memory and fantasy.

Finally, around two-thirty, she gave up the attempt at sleep and went back down to the living room. She switched on the word processor, popped in the floppy discs and waited while the machine loaded the Word-Star program she'd been using.

NAME OF FILE TO EDIT?

She typed in "MacCrory" and hit the return key. In milliseconds, the copy she'd created for the brochure advertising MacCrory Biotechnics' cross-country skiing simulator, "the home exercise machine for the eighties athlete," filled the screen with paragraph after paragraph of bright green letters.

She had breezed through the hard-sell portion of the brochure. Now all she had left were the specifications: the technical information on the thickness of the welded steel, construction of the frame—all the boring things she hated but did so well.

Her last assignment at DCH Prototypes before she was fired had consisted of translating convoluted technical jargon into a facsimile of plain English that a person without an advanced degree in electrical engineering could understand.

Katie had been highly respected in the firm. She'd been at the top of the pay scale; she'd had her own office, her own secretary, her own expense account. Four weeks' vacation, paid sick leave, enormous Christmas bonuses and a profit-sharing plan second to none.

Funny how it took being fired to show her just how much she'd hated that job.

Unlike many tech writers she knew, Katie had the ability to speak to the consumer, to make the most mundane item sound so appealing that the MasterCard was out before the buyer had a chance to think.

The job with Robert's firm offered her a chance to use none of those skills. It was technical writing at its most pure—and most boring. The lure of security, however, had been great, and before her trip to Tokyo she had been certain that she would accept the offer.

Now she wasn't certain about anything.

Since meeting Tom Sagan, she had drastically rearranged her old realities. She had discovered a capacity for joy that her disciplined nature had conveniently pushed aside.

Even the incident in what was once the nursery hadn't been enough to dampen the sense of wonder she was feeling. The pain had been there—sharp and fierce, as always—but something about the ease with which Tom seemed to understand her sorrow lessened the awkwardness of the moment.

Not that she thought he'd known pain like that himself. No one could be so totally at ease within himself, so happy, and still have intimate knowledge of sorrow. His golden good looks were an extension of his lighthearted nature. The result of a charmed life.

In all her years with Robert, she had never felt that sense of unbridled optimism, of pure delight, that she absorbed from Tom each time she saw him. He brought out in her a sense of adventure even Gwen couldn't match. Since that night on the mountainside in Hakone, she'd been moving just outside the boundaries of her normal world, unable—and unwilling—to find her way back inside.

Next week there would be time enough to offer herself up on the altar of practicality.

She would have lunch with Robert and Mr. Jameson, and her normal world would allow her to slip back within its boundaries once again.

She glanced at the blinking green cursor on her word processor's screen.

No more impossible deadlines, no more wondering what the next assignment would be, no more stacks of work piled up in her nice and tidy living room.

She'd say goodbye to Katie Powers, free-lance writer, and hello to Bernstein, Jameson and Coulter.

But that was next week.

She still had three and a half days with Tom Sagan ahead of her, three and a half days to explore the woman inside that she never knew existed.

Why not let responsibility and sorrow be damned, and take what he offered, and give what she could?

He talked a pretty story of love at first sight, but she wasn't foolish enough to believe that she would be more than a pleasant memory for him by this time next year.

Nothing in life lasted; that was a lesson she'd learned early on.

The secret was to take happiness where you could and not mourn its passing. She, more than many, understood how quickly sorrow could change everything.

In the scheme of things, three and a half days was but the blink of an eye. However, if she just let her heart run free, those three and a half days of happiness with Tom Sagan could warm her soul for a long time to come.

"Be daring," Gwen had said. "Live dangerously."

For once in her life, Katie was in full agreement with her sister.

It wasn't working.

From the moment Katie pulled up in front of the hotel in her black Mazda, Tom knew he was in deep water. The intimacy they'd shared the night before seemed to have vanished. She was breezy and friendly and funny, but as distant as the Milky Way. Katie had somehow donned her cool and logical persona once again, and he felt like tossing her over his shoulder and carrying her off to his room.

He wanted them to get to know each other.

She wanted him to get to know Boston.

Katie was as upbeat as a member of the chamber of commerce, and just as impersonal. If he hadn't known better, he would have thought he had imagined the wonders of the night before.

She dragged him from the USS *Constitution* to Old North Church to Boston Common and Faneuil Hall. It was a guided tour of the Revolutionary War complete with battle fatigue.

He began to wonder why England had fought so hard to retain these colonies. If all New Englanders were as single-minded and stubborn as Katie, he would have recommended fat King George hand them their independence and consider himself well out of it.

She was about to give him a tour of Harvard when it started to rain, and he somehow managed to convince her to come up with some indoor entertainment. Unfortunately, drinks at the top of the Prudential Tower downtown weren't exactly what he had in mind.

"To Boston," she said, raising her glass in a toast. "Isn't it wonderful?"

Tom clinked glasses with her and took a swig of Chivas-and-soda for fortification.

"Tom." Katie was nothing if not persistent. "Isn't Boston wonderful?"

He cleared his throat. "The view is terrific," he said, looking out the enormous window at the skyline.

"I don't mean the skyline."

He didn't think so. "I liked watching them rowing their boats on the Charles."

She laughed into her amaretto. "Sculls, Tom," she said. "Not rowboats."

"Whatever."

"That's all you liked?"

"The pizza at Faneuil Hall was damned good."

"I give you the four-star tour and all you liked was the pizza?"

"I told you I don't like Boston."

"What don't you like about it?" She fairly bristled with righteous hometown indignation.

"The same things I told you I didn't like last night. Crowds, noise, pollution." The memories of his time at Harvard had permanently ruined the city for him.

She finished her drink and stood up. "Why don't I just drive you back to your hotel and we can call it a night. I'd hate to bore you with a tour of Boston by lamplight."

Some of the flash and fire that made Katie so appealing resurfaced.

"Sit down."

"The hell I will." She pushed her thick red hair off her face. "You stand up. We're leaving."

He started to smile. "If I stand up, you'll regret it, Katie Powers."

"A threat?" Her eyes widened, but she stood her ground. No coward, she. Katie looked as if she were poised to do battle.

"No threats," he said. "Just this."

He rose from his seat. She took a step back, but he moved quickly. She was in his arms before she could form a protest, her mouth possessed by his.

Two couples at the bar broke into applause.

"You're insane!" Katie pulled slightly away from him. "Couldn't you wait, Tom?"

"We don't have time to wait," he said, noting the high color of her cheekbones, the dark smolder in her impossibly blue eyes.

"This is a public place!"

"I don't give a damn." He kissed her again. Someone at the bar whistled.

A smile hovered at the corners of her mouth but stubborn Katie refused to give in to it. "I'm leaving," she said, despite the fact that his arms were securely around her. "I refuse to be humiliated like this."

"I'm not humiliating you."

"People are staring at us."

He glanced around. "They're enjoying love in bloom."

"Yeah," called the bartender. "This is better than watching *Cheers*."

Katie turned and glared at the poor man. "Why don't you mind your own business?"

"Don't pick on him," Tom said. "You're mad at me, remember?" He tightened his grip on her.

"Let go of me, Tom."

"Will you sit back down?"

"No."

"Then I won't let go."

"I know karate, and I won't hesitate to use it."

"I'm a black belt," he answered. "I think I can handle myself."

"Damn it, Tom. Do you have to be so stubborn?"

"Yes." He kissed her forehead. "Face it, Katie. You're stuck with me until Sunday night."

The fire in her eyes turned into a sparkle. "You're impossibly pigheaded, did you know that?"

"So are you, lady."

"Never like this," she said, shaking her head. "I'm usually so levelheaded, so calm—you have a terrible effect on me, Sagan."

He released her from his arms and they both sat down, to the profound disappointment of the bartender and his customers.

"You keep telling me you're so calm and levelheaded. All I keep seeing is a woman with a temper like a Roman candle and more passion than she knows how to deal with."

She looked down at her glass. "I think we should decide where to go to dinner."

"To hell with dinner."

She looked back up at him, the expression on her face unreadable.

"It's not just because I hate Boston, is it?"

"No, it's not."

"All day I've felt as if you were slipping behind a stone wall."

She smiled. "You're too perceptive for your own good, Sagan."

"Tell me, Katie. Talk to me. If you don't level with me now, we'll never have a chance."

"I'm giving you as much as I can, Tom," she said, meeting his gaze. "More than that you don't have the right to ask for."

"Then you don't know me, because I want everything, Katie."

"You're going to have to settle for three days of my life."

"That's not enough."

"It will have to be, Tom."

"It's that or nothing?"

"For the moment." She finished her amaretto. "For all I know, you've tried this line on women from here to Tokyo and back."

The easy joke eluded him. "I have no business being here, Katie. This is as tough for me as it is for you." Molly's voice telling him to come back still lingered in his ears.

Katie hesitated so long that he thought all was lost.

"I've never felt less in control of my own life."

"I haven't been in control since the moment we met, Katie."

None of this was part of his plan, either. He should be back in Las Vegas right now getting geared up for the competition, not sitting in a bar in his least favorite city, trying to woo a reluctantly passionate redhead. That came too close to the kind of irresponsible behavior he had once been guilty of.

"What's happening between us scares the hell out of me, Tom."

"It scares hell out of me, too." He'd felt her drifting away from the moment he discovered she'd once had a child, and he was determined to catch her before she drifted too far.

"Things are moving too quickly. It's too soon—"

"Throw away your watch, Katie." He pressed his lips to the pulse point just beyond her wrist, savoring the scent of her skin. "Not everything in life follows a nice, polite schedule."

"I like order. Life should follow a pattern, a natural progression."

"We met, we talked, we've loved. A natural progression."

"A bit accelerated," she said. "We barely know each other."

"We'll get to know each other this weekend."

"But you hate Boston."

"I'll survive it."

"You hate crowds."

"I'll make a sacrifice."

She smiled and fire danced in her eyes. "We could go to my family's house on the Cape."

"I changed my mind. I still hate crowds." The last thing he wanted was to share her with her family.

"There won't be a crowd. Just you and me."

He thought of her house, where memories waited around every corner, where she could put up her barricade and hide when the emotional going got tough.

"No second thoughts?"

Her husky laugh sent a thrill through his body.

"A thousand second thoughts," she said, tossing him her car keys. "But right now none of them seems important."

For a second he wondered if he was crazy. Once he left that bar, there would be no turning back. The same insane emotion that had knocked him for a loop in Japan was sending him straight over the edge of reason right now.

There would be no turning back from Katie Powers.

Not in three days.

Not in three lifetimes.

8

The wall Katie had been erecting stone by stone all day crumbled before Tom's unblinking honesty. It was perfectly clear that her fate had been decided back on that mountainside in Japan, and any attempt on her part to change destiny was as futile as it was foolhardy.

Her last-ditch effort at escaping her own desires had failed gloriously. Surrender had never been so seductive.

"Come on," she said. "Let's go."

They stopped long enough for each to pack an overnight bag, then began the drive out to the Powers' home on the lower Cape.

Katie was feeling the aftereffects of her long night at the word processor and asked Tom to drive her Mazda. She regretted her decision before they were even out of the city proper.

"There is such a thing as a speed limit," she said as they whizzed past a family in a blue Oldsmobile station wagon.

"I'm not going that fast," he said as he claimed the left-hand lane.

She leaned over to look at the speedometer. He was indeed going only fifty-six miles per hour. "Maybe it's the lack of control that's so deceiving."

"I'm in control, Katie."

He was. It was Katie who wasn't.

"We're going to Hyannis, right?"

"Chatham," she corrected. "They sold the Hyannis house when I started high school."

"Your parents have money?"

"They're comfortable."

"My family is stinking rich."

She started to laugh. "Tom!"

"It's the truth," he said, laughing with her. "I'm just not good at your Yankee euphemisms."

"Is everyone in your family as blunt as you are?" He seemed so much an individual that it was hard to imagine the family structure that had created him.

"I'm the tactful one. My sister, Molly, makes me look like a diplomat."

"Your whole family is in the fireworks business?"

"Every last one of them." He slowed speed behind a motorcycle that was having difficulty in the heavy coastal rain. "I think it's a genetic trait. Molly's son was born on the Fourth of July and to celebrate we sent up a thousand split-tail comets."

"Is Molly's husband in the business?"

"No. Hugh's the only sane one. He's a computer whiz. We met in the navy and I introduced him to Molly and—"

"Fireworks?"

"Fireworks. I keep telling Molly I saved her from a life of spinsterhood and she should be grateful, but she gives me no respect at all."

"I think I like the sound of Molly."

"You two are a lot alike, actually. She has a hell of a temper, too."

"Maybe you bring it out in us," Katie said.

They bantered back and forth for a while as they neared the turnoff for Chatham. Strange, but the farther they got away from Boston, the more lighthearted Katie felt. The pulls and tugs of reality stretched and finally snapped, and a heightened sense of anticipation and desire took their place.

She looked over at Tom, whose classic profile was illuminated by the headlights of passing cars. The sight of him was enough to heat her blood to the danger point.

She had to face the unsettling fact that she, Kaitlin Anne Powers, was in love: head over heels, mindlessly, passionately, dangerously in love with a man with whom she had nothing in common.

But then, who said sharing common interests inevitably led to happiness?

She and Robert had been cut from the same cloth; their backgrounds, their points of reference, their goals in life all meshed perfectly. She had eased into married life without a ripple because the life she and Robert shared was the same life from which they had both been spawned.

Familiar. Conservative. Comforting.

And, she could admit now, strangely empty. When faced with real sorrow, real emotion, they retreated into their years of background and breeding and watched their marriage tumble like a house of cards.

Tom, with his offbeat personality and shoot-from-the-hip honesty, had made her laugh more in eight hours than she had laughed in eight years of marriage.

She thought of the intensity of the night before, an intensity that far transcended sex. What sprang to life between them when they met was as inexplicable as a shooting star, and just as beautiful. It needed no justification for being; the fact that it existed was enough.

Katie gave up searching for some handy Yankee euphemism to describe all she felt as she looked at him.

Love, improbable though it may be, seemed to say it best.

The heavy summer rain had turned into a full-fledged northeaster by the time Tom eased the Mazda over the soggy, unpaved driveway that wound its way up to her parents' summer home overlooking the ocean.

Not that he could see the ocean in the rain-swept blackness. He could barely see the driveway itself, despite the fact he had the high beams on. Only the salty sting of the air and the muffled roar told him that, somewhere close by, the Atlantic Ocean waited.

The Mazda went into a gentle skid and he eased it straight again. One more curve like that last one, and he and the Atlantic might be on intimate terms.

By the time he stopped near the side door of the house, he owed God, Lady Luck and two or three lesser-known saints his firstborn for getting Katie and him there in one piece.

"Is this retribution for bad-mouthing Boston?" he asked as they set their bags down in the hallway. "The Founding Fathers send down Hurricane Katie to blast me back to Vegas?"

Katie, her wet hair molded to her delicate skull, laughed out loud. "You have a lot to learn, Thomas." She closed, then bolted, the massive wooden door against the howling wind. "A hurricane would make this storm look like a gentle spring rain."

"Remind me to get out before hurricane season."

"Then you'd better get your plane ticket ready, because this is hurricane season."

He stripped off his sodden shirt and draped it over a railing where Katie had put her drenched sweater.

"Now I understand where you get your fierceness from. You're a product of your environment."

She seemed to enjoy the observation. "That's me. A tough old New Enlgander doing battle with the elements."

"Then come here, my tough New Englander," he said, opening his arms wide. "Come and do battle."

The storm outside swirled, then settled in the center of Katie's chest. Her heart thudded violently against her ribs, and she could feel the blood pounding in every pulse point in her body. Tom's naked torso, glistening with rain, was the most beautiful thing she'd ever seen.

"I'm a fighter," she said, holding her ground, "descended from a long line of fighters."

"You've been fighting this since the moment we met." He took a step toward her. "Come to me, sweet Katie. The battle awaits."

"You don't even know where the battleground is, Thomas."

"Don't I?" He moved closer still and put his hand over her heart. The heat from his body called up an answering heat inside her own.

He drew her into his arms, and she knew the battle was lost before it had begun.

She led him to the bedroom at the front of the house. The enormous windows were unshuttered, and it seemed as if they were suspended out over the ocean, with the rain and the wind and the lightning their only companions.

The sound of the ocean crashing against the rocks below unleashed the rest of her inhibitions. When Tom gently eased down the zipper of her blue-and-white sundress, she stepped out of it, then removed the last of her garments while he watched, his topaz eyes turning to molten gold.

"You wore that dress the day we met," he said as she helped him remove his clothing.

"I didn't think you'd remember."

"Not remember? I saw you on the platform and thought I'd never seen a woman more beautiful." He swept her up into his arms and carried her toward the antique brass bed by the window. "I wanted to push my way out of the train and carry you off to some mountain hideaway where I could make love to you all night."

"We have all night," she whispered as he lay down beside her. "All night and beyond."

Both, it turned out, were prepared this time.

He covered her body with his own and she sank deeper into both the soft mattress and fantasy. For endless minutes they lay perfectly still, drowning in the sensation of skin against skin; the only sounds in the room were those of the storm, their breathing and the wild pounding of their hearts.

She could feel him, hard and aroused, against her leg, but he made no move other than to cup her face between his massive hands. Her own hands feasted on the beautifully sinewed muscles of his back.

Desire burned inside her, yet was tempered by a fierce, unexpected tenderness that gathered strength with each moment. It seemed a thousand years since she'd touched and been touched with such sweet tenderness, such infinite joy.

She needed to show him how she felt; she needed to share with him the intense pleasure that coursed through her veins.

Her hands slid over his shoulders and down his arms, her sensitized skin memorizing the feel of warmth and restrained power. His breath drew in sharply when she traced a pattern across his flat belly, along the juncture of thigh and groin.

He trailed a finger down her throat and over her breasts, then moved lower.

With a soft laugh she angled just out of his reach while he stayed wonderfully within hers.

"If you keep doing that, sweet Katie, I won't be able to do all the things I've been dreaming of."

She pressed a kiss against his hipbone, savoring the clean, masculine smell of his skin. "Oh, yes, you will." Her mouth moved lower.

He groaned. "I'll need time."

She looked up and smiled, then unfastened the catch of her watch. "We have time," she said, dropping the watch to the floor. "All the time in the world."

If only that were true.

Hours later, Tom leaned over and retrieved the gold Rolex watch from the floor next to the bed. The crystal was cracked in two places. He held it to his ear. It was silent.

"I hope this is a quartz watch."

"Afraid not."

He put it on the nightstand next to her and pulled her back into his arms.

"It was a grand gesture, though, Katie. Very effective."

She laughed against his shoulder. "Glad you liked it."

"I especially liked it when you..." He whispered into her ear.

"I thought you would. I liked that, too. A watch is a small price to pay for such high drama."

"I'll buy you another one."

"I'd rather have that one fixed."

"Sentimental value?"

She met his eyes. "Now."

"We'll have it bronzed. We can set it on our mantel and tell the grandchildren about our night on the Cape."

He regretted his words as soon as they left his mouth. Her sudden tension was palpable beneath his hands.

"Let's spare the world the intimate details of our relationship, shall we?"

He recognized her attempt to keep the shadows at bay, and his heart went out to her.

"I'm a good listener," he said, stroking her hair.

"I'm fine."

"I'm not. That's the second time I've stumbled over the topic of children."

"You didn't stumble," she said, drawing away a fraction. "It's not a forbidden subject, Tom."

That damned wall was going up again, separating the two of them. He couldn't let it happen. "Her name was Jill, wasn't it?"

A flash of lightning outside the window illuminated Katie's face for an instant. He'd never forget the stricken expression in her eyes.

"How on earth do you know that?"

"In Hakone." He paused. "When you said 'God-speed.'"

"It's been three years." Her voice cracked on the last word but she quickly recovered. "It still sometimes sneaks up on me."

He thought about his own losses and how poignant the Daimonji Yaki, the fireworks display, had been for him as well.

"The torchlight ceremony was pretty damned effective, wasn't it?"

She nodded. "It left me feeling a little rocky, but I'll get over it."

"I'll repeat what I said before: If you feel like talking, I'm a good listener."

"Jill was two months old when she died. I have no anecdotes, no cute stories, not even a good reason for why it had to happen."

"Crib death?"

"They call it Sudden Infant Death Syndrome now, but it's still the same. One morning you go into your child's room and—" She stopped and turned on her side so she faced the window.

He put his hand on her shoulder and could feel the tremors shaking her slender body.

"I'm not crying."

"I never said you were, Katie."

"I never cried over Jill."

He thought of the day after the funeral when he drove way out into the Nevada desert and swore into the sun with rage and guilt over losing Paula and Buck.

"You should." He was a fine one to talk. The rage had disappeared, but the guilt remained.

She turned slightly and looked at him. "It's not that I don't want to," she said. "Every time I think I'll finally weep for her, something inside me balks at the thought of losing control."

"It's a release," he said, "not a loss of control."

"That's what everyone told me at the funeral. Do you know what it's like to stand at your daughter's graveside, dry-eyed, while your secretary sobs into her handkerchief? I was sure there was something terribly wrong with me."

He moved closer to her, wrapping his arms around her waist. Another flash of lightning illuminated the room for an instant, then faded. "How did your husband handle his grief?"

Her shoulders rose and fell in a shrug. "Personally. We each handled things in our own way."

Obviously, neither one had done a very good job of it, or they would still be married. That, of course, was something Tom could not say. A marriage like hers was as alien to him as snow was to the equator.

"Did you think about having another child?"

"Never. We barely thought of sex, much less conception."

He'd thought of little else but sex after the explosion. Night after night, he prowled the Dunes and the MGM Grand, taking mindless pleasure in all-too-willing flesh. It wasn't until he zeroed in on the competition that he'd been able to get some kind of perspective on his guilt.

As Katie already knew, surviving can be tragic in itself.

"Sorrow is an odd thing," he began, trying to choose the words that would give her the most comfort. "If you—"

She turned completely around, her body a silvery silhouette against the open window. "What do you know about sorrow, Thomas?'' She moved into his arms with fluid grace, wrapping her arms about his neck and ruffling his hair. "You've led a charmed life."

Exactly what he'd wanted her to think. That easygoing first impression had stood him in good stead over the years, providing a golden shield to hide his sorrows.

Why, now, did he want to lay it at her feet?

"Katie, I don't think I—"

She kissed him soundly. "You talk too much. We've wasted far too much time talking."

Before he could say anything more, she eased him back down into that incredible mattress. It would have been an easy thing to stop her magic hands.

It would have been an easy thing to turn this moment into something deeper.

But she moved her body against his and made sure— in a very imaginative way—that he couldn't talk for a long, long time.

He was a dangerous man.

Katie turned over and looked at Tom, who slept with one leg outside the covers and one arm around her. Although it was the middle of the night, the storm had broken momentarily, and enough starlight shone through the window for her to be able to savor his extraordinary good looks.

With his head of curly blond hair, he seemed a fallen angel. That bushy mustache above his full mouth, the angles and planes of his cheekbones and jaw provided a counterpoint of toughness, of male power, to his classically handsome face.

She gently pushed a lock of hair off his forehead and felt sudden tears burn against her eyes.

Ah, yes, he was a dangerous man.

His kind of danger had nothing to do with the obvious lure of sex or money or power. Katie could have handled those temptations quite handily.

Tom Sagan's type of danger was much more subtle, much more seductive. What he did was cast light into the hidden corners of her heart, drawing her secret sorrows, her private fears out of darkness.

It was something she and her ex-husband had never been able to manage.

"Talk about her," the therapist had said to Kaitlin and Robert Morrisson one month after their daughter had died. "Don't keep things bottled up inside."

Kaitlin and Robert had come to the therapist at the urging of Robert's parents, who felt uneasy about the couple's stoicism.

"Talk about Jill's death," the therapist urged. "Talk about how it makes you feel."

Bob was the first one to speak. "There's nothing to say, is there? Nothing we can say or do will bring her back."

Katie looked at her husband and nodded. "We've made our peace with it. Why dredge up old memories?"

"Old memories?" the therapist asked. "It's been only a month, Kaitlin. The mourning process is much slower than that. Your grief is still fresh. Your memories are still vital."

"We're fine," Bob said. "We've accepted our loss."

"Yes," Katie said. "Why can't everyone understand that we're fine?"

They had given away the furniture in the nursery, covered up the Disney mural with Laura Ashley wall-

paper, then returned to being a couple after a taste of
being a family, all before the month was out.

Jill's short life and unexpected death had left no
outward signs behind. Katie had made sure that the al-
bums of photos from the hospital and the christening
were hidden away in the attic with the baby shoes.

The only time the reality of what had happened hit
her was when she took a shower and the faint, pale
marks on the outer curves of her breasts and on her flat
stomach reminded her of what had been.

The therapist had sighed and pushed her glasses to the
top of her head. "I'm here if you want to talk," she
said, rising to shake her hands. "Needing someone to
talk to isn't a sign of weakness."

Six months later, Katie remembered those words.

She and Bob, always so much alike, had each retreated into their own careers, their own pain, and what
had once been a functioning marriage was now more
like a business arrangement.

Sometimes the need to talk about Jill swept over her
and she would turn to Bob in the night, only to find him
inarticulate in his own grief.

And when the same need engulfed Bob, Katie found
it impossible to speak of their daughter.

They shared the same sorrow, but found it impossible to bring comfort to each other. In a bizarre parody
of intimacy, grief for their lost child bound them together, yet kept them apart.

Katie quickly grew accustomed to bypassing her sorrow, deftly sidestepping her memories of Jill.

It was a skill that had served her well.

At least, it had until that magical night at the base of
Mount Myojo, when Tom Sagan exploded into her life
like a Saturn Star and threw open the door to her heart.

Tom stirred and she moved closer to him. The sound of his heartbeat echoed in her head as she curved her body against his. She watched as a slight smile tilted the corners of his dark blond mustache.

Even his dreams were touched by magic.

Lucky man never to have known the dark side of fate.

Tom awoke once near dawn to the sound of the storm outside his window and the crashing of the waves against the rocks below.

Lightning streaked across the sky, its power both awesome and beautiful.

For one terrible moment, he was back in time to another summer night.

The night they had tried to outdo the gods of darkness, and the gods decided to remind the mortals exactly who ruled both the heavens and hell.

Katie slept beside him, her body silhouetted against the white sheets and blanket.

She saw him as he wanted her to see him—as fortune's child grown to adulthood without ever knowing the back of Fate's hand.

He'd chosen to show her only the golden side of his life. Why, then, did her ready acceptance bother him so much?

He knew her name, her sister's name, her birthday. He knew where she lived, how she worked, how she played. In one day, he had absorbed images of her as a child and incorporated them with his image of the woman she had become.

What had started as a crazy, lovesick quest, certain to burn out more quickly than a soaring comet, had turned into something different.

He had arrived at Logan Airport not knowing exactly what to expect. He'd hoped for magic, but would have settled for memories.

Now he was afraid memories were all he'd take back with him to Las Vegas.

The real Katie remained as elusive as the perfect blue flame.

And twice as dangerous.

9

When Tom woke up just before noon, it was still raining. Not the violent storm of the previous night, but a steady, gray stream of rain that made it impossible to distinguish sky from ocean.

Katie, dressed in a worn Harvard sweatshirt and tight, faded jeans, sat curled up on the window seat, sipping a cup of what he hoped was strong coffee.

"It's about time," she said as he sat up and raked his hair off his forehead. "We Yankees don't take kindly to indolence."

He started to swing his legs out of the bed but suddenly became self-conscious about his condition: naked and aroused. He stifled a yawn instead. "It's not indolence; it's jet lag. Is that coffee you have there?"

"Lipton tea. The house has been empty all summer. We're out of almost everything."

"I'd kill for a cup of coffee."

"I think there's some instant."

"As I said, I'd kill for a cup of coffee."

He was trying to think of a way to grab his pants from the chair across the room without making a major production of it when Katie got up from the window seat and handed him his clothes.

"The temperature dropped twenty-five degrees overnight. You'd better dig out something long-sleeved."

He thought of the dry desert heat back home and shook his head. "New England summer, huh? I'm not impressed, Katie."

She picked up a pillow from the chaise lounge across the room and tossed it at him.

"You have to be tough to live in New England, Sagan," she said, laughing as he grabbed the pillow just before it hit the nightstand. "Stay here awhile and I'll make a man out of you yet."

The look in her eyes made the air between them sizzle. He kicked the bedcovers on the floor and stood up.

She looked at him, then looked again. "Well," she drawled as he crossed the room to claim her, "looks like someone beat me to it."

Katie insisted that he see Provincetown, or "P-town," as she called it, and they drove through the rain to the eastern tip of the Cape. Despite the bad weather, tourists filled the crafts shops and schlocky souvenir stores, while the locals wisely kept out of the rain in the many cafés.

Despite his Vegas upbringing, the first time he saw two men dressed in identical yellow rain slickers, strolling down the street hand in hand beneath an enormous raspberry-colored golf umbrella, he stared like a rube, and Katie had to pinch his arm to bring him back to normal.

"Now I understand that street sign we saw by the parking lot," he said, shaking his head. "Provincetown *does* go both ways, doesn't it?"

She laughed and led him into a tiny restaurant near the pier where the Greenpeace ships went out on the whale watches.

"I hope that punctured some of your preconceived notions about staid New Englanders, Mr. Sagan."

They took a seat near the window and he glanced around at the clientele. A blond man near the counter winked at him, and Tom, his face burning, turned back to Katie. He would never doubt Yankee ingenuity again. . . .

A waitress in a black vinyl miniskirt that looked suspiciously like a Hefty bag took their orders for clam chowder and crinkled back toward the kitchen.

"This is a hell of a far cry from Boston. Are you sure we're in the same state?" He shook his head. "Hell, are you sure we're in the same country?"

He loved it when she laughed. "This is my favorite place on the Cape," she said, popping an oyster cracker into her mouth. "You can be exactly who you are—no explanations necessary."

He arched a brow. "I thought you were a dyed-in-the-wool Bostonian, pedigree and all."

Her impossible blue eyes twinkled. "Can I let you in on a secret?" He nodded. "I don't like Boston, either."

He couldn't have been more surprised if she had told him she was a practicing voodoo priestess. "You love Boston! The Common, the river, the Old North Church. Wasn't it you who gave me the six-hour guided tour of your hometown's wonders?"

"I was as bored as you were, Tom."

"I wasn't bored," he lied.

She raised an eyebrow at him. "You dozed off during that educational movie at Faneuil Hall."

"I was resting my eyes."

"You snored."

"A sinus condition." He started to laugh. "You were really bored?"

"Terminally."

"I'm finding this hard to believe, Katie. Aren't you the one who defended Boston like this was 1776 and I was King George?"

"A good citizen always defends her hometown, doesn't she? Actually I'd prefer not to live in the city."

"So what's holding you back?"

"Work."

"If you work for yourself, you can live anywhere." She'd told him about the amount of traveling she'd done during these past four months of free-lance work. "Your home base doesn't have to be in Boston."

"That's only valid if I work for myself," she said, glancing out the window. "If I take the job with B, J and C, I'm tethered to Boston."

"Don't take the job."

"Easy for you to say."

The waitress deposited big bowls of New England clam chowder in front of them and disappeared again.

"It's not like you have no alternatives, Katie. You told me your free-lancing has really taken off."

She sampled her soup before answering. "It has, but there's no guarantee I'll still be in business this time next year."

"Life doesn't come with guarantees."

"I like to control as many of the variables as I can, Tom. What if my business failed?"

"I've seen your home—you're in no danger of bankruptcy. People with a hell of a lot more to lose take chances every day."

"Haven't we been over this territory before? I like security."

"The hell you do, Katie Powers," he said, leaning across the small table. "You like a challenge even more."

Katie stared at him. The soup spoon dangled foolishly from her fingers. Either the man was psychic, or she had revealed more to him in their few days together than she had to anyone else in her entire life.

"Did I tell you that?"

"You didn't have to. A fool could see you're dying to tackle life head-on."

"I know a lot of people with IQs in the stratosphere, Tom, and not one of them ever thought of me as a risk-taker."

"Then they didn't look closely enough. You're a risk-taker, Katie—a frustrated one, perhaps, but a risk-taker."

Suddenly she felt exposed, as if an X-ray machine were trained on her heart, and she laughed nervously. "Who would guess that beneath this Harvard sweatshirt hid the woman of steel?"

He took her hand. "I would."

His touch sent off little tremors inside her. "You're unnerving me, Thomas. I'm not used to such undivided attention."

"You're not used to someone who can see over that wall you've put up around yourself."

Unbelievable. He'd even zeroed in on her own metaphor. She looked out the window and watched the rain-soaked tourists wobble down the gangplank of the Greenpeace ship on the other side of the dock. "Do I talk in my sleep?"

"You're simply not that hard to read, my tough Yankee."

"No one's ever been able to do it before."

He took her hand and kissed the palm. "Maybe you never wanted anyone to be able to before."

She met his eyes. "Do you think it's something I can control?"

"We all can, Katie, to one extent or another. We all determine who we let inside our hearts."

She thought of the way he had followed her halfway around the world. "I don't recall having any choice in the matter," she said, smiling.

Those golden eyes of his grew serious. "You always have a choice," he said, sitting back. "Don't ever think otherwise."

She wanted to make a joke about his showing up on her Beacon Hill doorstep ready to carry her off into the night, but the words died in her throat. She, a woman who'd always wanted total control of her actions, had been trying to hide behind the notion of being swept away by a man's passion.

Nice idea, but it wasn't going to work.

Not this time.

Tom Sagan may have set everything in motion, but Katie still had the power to stop things anytime she wanted to.

The only problem was she didn't want to.

She had the rest of her life to worry about jobs and security and pension plans for her old age. Magic happened only once, if a woman was lucky, and she intended to enjoy the magic while it lasted.

Sunday night would be there soon enough.

She thought of her broken watch, which rested, silent and still, on the nightstand back at the house in Chatham.

If only it were really that easy to stop time.

By late afternoon, the storm finally blew out to sea, and Tom had to admit that a Cape Cod sunset was something to behold.

He and Katie were stretched out on an enormous chaise lounge on the deck of her parents' beach house, watching the Atlantic blaze like liquid fire as the sun began its descent. Down on the beach, some teenagers were setting off small rockets, and with each explosion he felt the pulls and tugs of responsibility calling him home.

Had life ever been as simple as he remembered? Had he ever really believed he was free to pick up and go, the way he had at nineteen when he had dropped out of Harvard and set out to see America?

Even then as he bummed around, doing odd jobs here and there, he'd been connected to his family, to his past, as surely as if he were still under their roof. The connection was in his blood and in his bone; his father's passions and ideals had somehow become his own.

And he had to prove to himself just once that he was worthy of that honor. Only then would he be free to let Katie see his secret, hidden heart.

"Don't they ever get tired of it?" Katie's voice was low and lazy. "Why don't they try volleyball for a while?"

Tom said nothing. He watched with envy as they dug the mortars in, then touched off another shell with a railroad flare. A break, then a report issued from the shell, followed by a thump of propellant charge that drove the shell out of the mortar.

The rocket whistled past the deck, then popped as the canister opened a few yards away. A curved spray of red and amber drizzled back down to the beach below.

"A far cry from Hakone, isn't it?" Katie said.

Tom gathered her into his arms. Her hair was as fiery as the setting sun. "They're not old enough yet to appreciate beauty."

"Spoken like a true professional." She kissed him on the jaw. "Are you thinking about your competition?"

"I was thinking I'd better call Molly tonight. If she doesn't make sure they have the shells made, we're in big trouble."

"I thought your family just put the shows together, not the fireworks themselves."

"Hell, no, Katie. We start from the ground up."

He thought of their compound, where twelve bunkers filled with the most powerful explosives imaginable rested uneasily in the middle of the desert outside Las Vegas. One simple twelve-inch shell took fifteen man-hours. They needed twenty thousand of them.

Wiring those shells would be a tedious, dangerous job. He would make sure every last one of them was aced before he let them out of the shop.

There wasn't time for any screwups.

Or side trips to New England.

Or falling in love.

"Let's go back to Boston in the morning," he said suddenly.

"But you hate Boston."

"Exactly."

"I thought we'd stay here until Sunday when you leave."

"Change of plans, Katie. Let's go back."

There, hidden away in that old beach house, it was too easy to forget the debts he had to repay. He was losing his edge, and that could spell disaster.

For his father, for Paula, for himself—he had to get back home.

He knew that if he stayed in Katie's arms much longer, he'd never be able to leave her.

And, unfortunately, leaving Katie was the first thing he had to do before he would be free to give her his heart.

Katie watched as he checked his suitcase at the desk and got his boarding pass at the airport Sunday night. Somehow she'd never believed this moment would come. Now that they were in the middle of it, she wondered how she could have ever been so naive.

To hell with you, Tom Sagan.

To hell with living dangerously.

To hell with love at first sight.

To hell with half-baked cli
éd ideas of fun with no strings that improbable men like Tom propagated on cool and logical women like Katie.

Following her halfway around the world had been a grand gesture, she'd grant him that. Only a man who lived a charmed life would ever have attempted something so flamboyantly romantic.

What amazed Katie was that she had bought it all. It wasn't until she got off the highway at the exit for Logan that she realized heartbreak was the flip side of grand gestures—the side that no one ever bothered to talk about.

These four days with Tom Sagan had shown her just how arid, how narrow, her life before him had been.

Against her will he'd burst into her life and pulled her headlong back into the mainstream, forcing her to acknowledge the truth about what she really needed to make her happy.

She would never again be able to pretend that she didn't want another chance at happiness.

She would never be able to pretend that she didn't want him.

But it didn't really matter, did it? It was Sunday night, and he had a plane to catch.

A little thing like love certainly wasn't going to slow him down.

Tom walked over to where she stood leaning against a pillar, guarding his carry-on luggage. Smart man to pick someone as well-mannered as she. Another woman might have checked his luggage onto the next plane to Timbuktu.

"Good timing," he said, flashing his boarding pass. "Last window seat, no-smoking section."

"Lucky you."

He picked up his bag. "It doesn't board for another thirty minutes."

She said nothing. There was no way she would make this easy for him.

"Want to sit in the bar?"

"If you like."

She'd nurse a club soda and a breaking heart and wonder why she'd been so quick to let him explode into her life like one of those damned shooting stars he talked so much about.

She glanced up at his handsome face, the beautiful, untroubled face of one of life's chosen ones.

To hell with him.

She'd managed just fine before Tom Sagan. She'd manage just as well after.

She followed him into the bar.

Katie sat opposite him at the small Formica table, fiddling with the red swizzle stick in her glass of club soda. Her jaw was set in that stubborn line he'd first noticed on the train in Hakone.

This was not the goodbye scene he'd imagined. But then again, nothing about the last twenty-four hours had been the way he'd imagined.

First, they'd overslept, not awakening until early afternoon—which wasn't surprising after the incredible night of passion they'd shared.

Then he'd had to go over to the Westin, where he'd stupidly provided most of his luggage with the luxury of a two-bedroom suite. Katie had been snappish and distant, and the perfect moment to tell her all he felt about her, all he wanted for the future, simply never arrived.

He glanced at his watch.

He had twenty-two minutes and a handful of seconds until the plane boarded, and not a hell of a lot of optimism.

"This isn't really goodbye, you know."

She looked up at him, her expression guarded. Only the fierce glint in her eyes gave her temper away.

Maybe there was still hope, after all.

"Las Vegas isn't that far away," he continued, proceeding cautiously. "As soon as the competition is over, you can come out and—"

"No."

"No?"

"I have no intention of coming to Las Vegas, Tom."

"It's not that wicked a place," he said, forcing a smile.

"Let me rephrase that: I have no intention of coming to Las Vegas to see you."

Eighteen minutes and counting.

"If I could handle four days in Boston, the least you could do is give Vegas a shot."

"Forget it."

"What the hell do you mean, forget it? Damn it, Katie, I followed you halfway around the world for a reason!"

"And we both know what that reason was, don't we?"

"Out West we shoot people for statements like that."

She glared at him, her blue eyes blazing. "You can drop that cowboy routine, Sagan. I'm on to you."

"If you think I came thousands of miles just to get you into bed, you're dead wrong. I want more than your body, Katie—I want the whole damned package."

Two blue-haired matrons at the next table stopped sipping their martinis and stared openly.

A month ago Katie would have disappeared beneath the tablecloth and crawled out of the bar in humiliation. That, however, was before she met Tom Sagan.

"If you don't mind, ladies, this is a private conversation."

They turned back to their drinks in a righteous huff.

Tom gave her the thumbs-up sign. "Good going, my fierce New Englander. I knew you had it in you."

She pulled her chair closer to the table and leaned across it. She wanted to make sure he heard everything she had to say—loud and clear.

He was still smiling at her, but he wouldn't be smiling after she was finished.

"Do you know what you are, Tom Sagan?" She didn't wait for a reply. "You're a selfish bastard."

The smile was already fading.

"How dare you show up on my doorstep and turn my life upside down! Whatever gave you the idea you had the right to follow me home and grab four days of my life without so much as an 'It's been nice'?" She grabbed her purse from the table and stood up. "I may have made one mistake with you, Tom, but I'll be damned if I make a second one. Goodbye."

The adrenaline was flowing so fast, she thought she could fly to Vegas and back under her own steam. She was out the door and into the corridor in the blink of an eye.

"Katie, wait!" Tom's steps pounded behind her.

She broke into a trot, dodging a collision with a worker waxing the tiled floor.

She was fast, but he was faster. He caught up to her near the ticket counter.

"You have to listen to me, Katie." He gripped her arm.

She tried to pull away but failed.

"If you won't come to me, I'll come back for you."

"I don't want to hear it," she said, finally yanking her arm away from him and heading for the door. "If you think I'm going to sit here waiting patiently for you, you're insane." There'd been no promises of a future, no plans. She certainly wasn't about to sign on as anyone's mistress—not even the mistress of the man she loved.

She pushed open the door and was about to leave when he grabbed her from behind and flipped her over his shoulder.

"You're going to listen to me, Katie, if I have to rope and tie you to a chair in the waiting room to do it."

It was hard to be dignified riding backward through the waiting room at Logan Airport, but she gave it her best shot. Even the security guards, damn their scurvy souls, looked amused.

"Put me down," she hissed into his ear. "My hands are lethal weapons and I can knock you from here to Chicago if I want to."

He didn't slow his step. "Give it your best shot, Powers. You're still going to listen to me."

He didn't put her down until they reached a tiny, deserted hallway near a recently bankrupted commuter airline. He deposited her on a rigid plastic chair, and although he didn't rope and tie her, his overpowering presence towering over her kept her in her seat.

Obviously there were sides to his personality she'd never seen.

"Flight 126, nonstop Logan to McCarran International, boarding Gate Fifteen," the scratchy voice on the loudspeaker announced.

"You'll miss your plane," she said.

"I'll take my chances."

He bent down in front of her so his eyes were level with hers.

"I'm coming back, Katie," he said. "I'm coming back to marry you."

She tried to jump up but he put his hand on her shoulder. "The hell you are!"

"As soon as the competition is over, I'm taking the next flight out for Boston."

"Then you'd better learn to like the city, because I'll be damned if I sit here waiting for you."

"There's no sense fighting it, Katie. We're in the hands of Fate."

To her embarrassment, tears began to well up.

"Leave me alone, Tom, please. I'm no good at playing these games. If it's over, just say so. I can handle it."

"Ah, yes. My strong New Englander."

She watched as he slipped off the heavy onyx-and-gold ring he wore on his right ring finger, then pressed it into her hand. It was still warm from his flesh.

"My pledge, Katie. I love you."

"I don't want it."

"Keep it anyway. I'll be back to replace it with a wedding ring."

"Dramatic gestures don't always work, Tom, not even for you golden boys. Maybe just this once you won't get your own way."

He pulled her to her feet and into his arms. A look of vulnerability tinged with pain flickered across his eyes, but it had disappeared before she could decide if it was real or imagined.

"Maybe not," he said as he tilted her chin up to him, "but it's a chance I have to take."

The sweetness of his kiss mingled with the bitter taste of her tears.

"Last call for Flight 126 to Las Vegas. All passengers report immediately to Gate Fifteen."

"I love you," she said as he released her from his embrace.

"Then wait for me, Katie. I'll be back. I promise."

He turned and walked down that long corridor without a backward glance.

10

August 31 Las Vegas

"You look like hell."

It was after two in the morning when Tom's plane landed in Las Vegas. Molly's cheerful greeting was not the welcome he'd been expecting.

"Good to see you, too." Tom kissed his sister and tossed his luggage into the back of her bright red Chevy Blazer.

Molly was a foot shorter than Tom but she made up for it in spirit. "You look like you haven't slept in a week."

"Try four and a half days."

They climbed into the four-wheel-drive vehicle and she pushed back into the crazy airport traffic. Tom took a gulp of coffee from the thermos that the caffeine-addicted Molly always kept by her side.

"Out with it." Molly leaned on the horn and cut off a shuttle bus on its way to the Avis Rent A Car building on the outskirts of the airport complex.

"Your driving stinks."

"I already know that. What on earth were you doing in Boston?"

"I don't remember." He took another sip of coffee. "Is the first tier of shells ready?"

She glanced at him, narrowly missing a crater-sized pothole on the access road. "I don't remember."

"I'm too tired to argue, Mol," he said, getting as comfortable as his seat belt would allow. "Did you get the material from Crown?"

"If you'd bothered to call again, you'd know the answer."

As if he didn't feel guilty enough as it was. "I had something else on my mind."

"We not only finished the first tier, brother dear, but we're halfway done with the second."

"Give up your painting, Mol. We could use you full-time."

"I'm not Maycee's daughter for nothing, am I?"

Their mother was Maycee Lewis, whose books on household hints and offbeat domestic efficiency had kept her consistently at the top of the best-seller lists. Molly had inherited their mother's knack for managing time and motion—a gift that blended strangely with her artistic talent.

The bright lights of the Vegas strip stood out against the unyielding desert darkness. He could pick out the red and gold of the Riviera and the flash of white from Caesar's Palace as they rode away from town.

He let his head fall back against the headrest and closed his eyes.

"Oh, no, you don't." Molly's voice caught him just before he drifted into sleep. "I'm not letting you out of this truck until you tell me what you've been up to."

"I'll tell you tomorrow." He closed his eyes again.

Molly switched on the interior lights. "You'll be buried up to your eyeballs in work tomorrow. Maycee and Ed and the rest of them are ready to pounce on you as soon as we pull into the driveway. Tell me tonight."

He groaned. "Now I know why poor Hugh always looks exhausted. You're nagging him to death."

"Hugh looks exhausted because he works twenty-two hours a day," Molly snapped back. "And don't try to change the subject."

"You're the second-most pigheaded woman I've ever known."

Molly turned to stare at him, and the Blazer veered off the road. Tom had to yank the steering wheel to get them back on track.

"I was in first place a month ago," Molly said. "What happened?"

He flipped off the overhead interior light so she wouldn't see the look on his face. "Sorry, Mol, but you've been bumped down to the second spot."

His sister might be stubborn and argumentative, but she wasn't stupid.

"You've fallen in love!"

"Surprised?"

Molly hooted with laughter. "Only that it's taken you this long. Who is she? Where did you meet her? Don't tell me in Boston, because I'll—"

"Her name is Katie Powers. I met her on a railway in Japan. And yes, she lives in Boston."

"It must be serious. You'd rather be trapped with a lounge act at the Dunes than spend time in Boston."

"Funny thing, Mol—Boston's not so bad."

"So where is she?"

"Back in Boston."

Once again Molly took her eyes from the road to stare at him.

"When's the wedding?"

"I don't know if there's going to be one."

"But you love her?"

"Yep."

Molly was quiet for a moment. "She doesn't love you."

"She loves me." He couldn't let himself think otherwise.

"You just want a casual affair?"

There was nothing casual about his feelings for Katie Powers. "I want to grow old and gray with her."

"She's not married, is she?"

"Divorced."

"Children?"

He thought of the shadowy Disney figures in what was once Jill's nursery. "None."

"You've made plans to see her again, of course."

"Afraid not."

Molly was having a terrible time keeping the truck on the road. Finally, she pulled off onto the soft shoulder and turned off the engine.

"Come on, Molly. It's after two in the morning. I want to get home."

"And I want some answers. No one meets a woman in Japan, follows her to Boston, then doesn't make plans to see her again. If this is some kind of joke, I don't think it's very funny."

Neither did he. "Do you see me laughing?"

"You might as well be, big brother," she said, dangling the truck's keys out of his reach. "Otherwise, we'll be here all night."

"Hugh will be worried about you."

"Hugh is in Cincinnati at a symposium."

"Settle down, Mol," he said, leaning back against the door of the Blazer, "and I'll tell you the story of Tom and Katie. Once upon a time..."

"And that's it?" Molly asked fifteen minutes later when Tom finished with an expurgated version of his romance with Katie Powers. "Where's the happily ever after?"

I wish I knew. "I don't know if there's going to be one." He stifled a yawn with the back of his hand. "It's up to Katie now."

"I should take you back to McCarran and put you on the next plane to Boston." Molly put the keys back into the ignition and started up the truck. "You should sit on her doorstep until you get things worked out."

"I can't, Molly. You know that."

"That damned stupid competition?"

"The competition."

"You're a fool, Tom," she said as they started back toward his house once more. "Fools rarely get a second chance."

Tom, however, said nothing. He closed his eyes and thought of Katie Powers with her fine temper and sharp wit and a loneliness that matched his. Asking her to come to him had been the act of a desperate man. She had come as far as she could, given as much as she was able.

Just because he came from a family of men and women who thrived on love at first sight didn't mean that logical Katie was able to toss caution to the four winds and join lives with him after less than a week.

Flamboyant gestures came easily to him. It was the more intimate act of sharing his pain that he found difficult.

He was glad Katie hadn't called his bluff and boarded the plane with him.

He needed space to breathe, time to think. What he had to do now had nothing to do with Katie Powers. He had an old score to settle with himself, and he didn't need the woman he loved to bear witness to his shortcomings.

He glanced at the bare spot on his finger where the onyx-and-gold ring had been. That ring had been Buck's, the only thing to survive the hideous explosion that took both his life and Paula's.

Maycee had given it to him the day of the funeral, and it hadn't left his finger until he gave it to Katie Powers in the middle of the airport, in what had to be the most unromantic, damn-fool proposal in the history of the Western world.

He had made a pledge to Katie, and he was a man of his word.

When it was all over, when the competition had come and gone and he'd made peace with himself by honoring Buck and Paula, he'd ask Molly to take him back to McCarran Airport, where he'd board the next plane to Boston and camp out on Katie's doorstep until she promised to marry him.

And if she didn't—well, being the descendant of a long line of cowboys and desperadoes had certain advantages.

He wouldn't think twice about throwing Katie over his shoulder once again and whisking her back to Cape Cod and that wonderful bedroom overlooking the ocean, where he could—

"...and if you don't, I'll do it for you." Molly's voice dragged him out of his fantasy. "Just give me her phone number."

"Molly," he said, sinking down into his seat and closing his eyes, "mind your own business."

Katie and Gwen had been on the telephone for one hour and forty-five minutes and they'd barely scratched the surface.

"AT&T should grant me shares as a bonus," Katie said as Gwen paused in her analysis of Katie's future. "I'm a natural resource."

"Better you than me," Gwen said, her voice remarkably clear despite the distance separating them. "I'm still a struggling translator."

"And I'm the one who's unemployed," Katie shot back, picking up her second can of Tab. "You should take pity on your younger sister."

"The hell I should. You're making more money freelancing than you ever did at your old job. You even have that juicy offer from Robert's company, though God knows why you'd be interested in that. I'd say your professional prospects are pretty rosy."

Katie was pretty sure she would be refusing the offer from Bernstein, Jameson and Coulter, but didn't feel like going into it right then. She had other, more important topics on her mind.

"Question: Why am I so miserable?"

"You needed to call me long-distance for that? You're in love. Being miserable is par for the course."

In the days since Tom returned home to Las Vegas, Katie had tried to come up with every reason known to man or woman to explain away the loneliness she felt.

Gwen, in her infinite wisdom, zeroed in on the explanation with laser-beam precision.

"Were you miserable when you met Hiro?"

"Of course I was. How else would I know it's real? Heartache is half the fun."

"I was never miserable with Robert."

"I rest my case."

Gwen's theory was getting interesting.

"We were happy together," Katie said slowly. "If it hadn't been for—"

"No, honey," Gwen broke in. "Even if Jill had lived, you and Bob wouldn't have lasted."

"I resent that."

"You know I'm right. Sooner or later, one of you would have realized there's more to life than a joint tax statement and an annuity."

"We loved each other, Gwendolyn. We were committed to our marriage." Why did her words sound as empty as her heart felt without Tom?

"You grew up together, then fell into marriage as easily as most people fall into a king-size bed. You did what was logical, Katie. You did what was expected. You married your friend, not your lover."

"I didn't think the two concepts were mutually exclusive."

"They're not," Gwen shot back, "but think of how wonderful marriage can be if you find a man who can be both."

The vivid image of Tom Sagan came immediately to mind. "It's a bit tough when the man in question lives two thousand miles away, Gwen."

"At last!" It wasn't hard to imagine the smile on her sister's face. "So now we finally get down to business. So you admit you're in love with Tom Terrific?"

Tom was terrific, all right, but Katie wasn't about to expound to her sister on just how terrific. "Yes, I am."

"What's the next step, then?"

Katie quickly filled Gwen in on the last conversation she and Tom had shared.

"...so he went back for the competition. End of story."

"Why is it so important to him?"

"Family honor, I suppose. Public relations."

She explained that it was an international competition that carried with it a lot of prestige within the pyrotechnic community.

"Why do I get the feeling there's more to it than that?" Gwen paused. "When did you say his father died?"

"I didn't. I never thought to ask."

"Do you think there's a connection between the competition and his father? A deathbed promise, perhaps?"

Katie twisted around in her desk chair, trying to find a comfortable position. "I never asked him anything about it."

"You spend a week with the man, and you never asked him about the competition that brought him all the way to Japan?"

"He was spying on his rivals," Katie said, feeling extremely uneasy. "Trying to get a jump on them."

"You're a fool, Kaitlin Powers. No one travels thousands of miles to watch a fireworks display unless that's the most important thing on earth to him. Didn't that tell you something about what motivates this man?"

Katie said nothing. She'd been so spellbound by the magic of that night in Hakone, so head over heels in love with his physical splendor, and—she hated to admit—so caught up in her private sorrow, that she'd never given it any thought.

Gwen hadn't missed a beat. "And then he puts all of that aside to follow you halfway around the world? My God, Katie! Where are your brains?"

Katie's answer was not fit for polite company.

"Do they give awards for stupidity?" she asked.

"If they did, you'd win hands down."

"Nothing like having your sister in your corner."

"Someone has to set you straight."

"So what do I do now?"

"He made the first move, Katie, and it was a winner. Why don't you make the next one?"

Katie looked out the window at the quiet, tree-lined street. A young couple in cutoffs and T-shirts were washing a BMW while an elderly couple strolled down the sidewalk hand in hand.

"Katie?" Gwen's voice was softer, more concerned than angry.

"Something is holding me back, Gwen," she said, turning away from the window. "Three times I picked up the telephone to call him, and each time my hand shook too much to dial his number."

"Ask for Operator Assistance."

"I'm serious, Gwen."

"I know what it is."

"If you do, then tell me, because I'm in the dark."

"When is your meeting with Robert and his boss?"

"Friday. What on earth does that have to do with anything?"

"Maybe you two still have some unfinished business. I'll call you Friday night and you can tell me if I'm right."

"Gwen, wait. I—"

Gwen hung up before Katie could finish her sentence.

"Damn it!" Katie slammed the phone down. Gwen had been living in the Orient too long. She was beginning to sound as mystical and mysterious as Hiro did after too much sake.

Unfinished business with Robert Morrisson? Absurd. The only unfinished business she had was with Bernstein, Jameson and Coulter, and by Friday that would be decided, one way or the other.

Robert was a friend, an associate, the conduit between her and B, J and C, and nothing more.

The love between them had died even before their marriage did, and all that remained was affection and respect and memories of the time they'd shared. She didn't feel the slightest twinge of jealousy when she saw Robert and Sunny together. The fact that he had taken that leap of faith a second time filled Katie with admiration.

And if the thought of their newborn daughter occasionally brought a pang of envy—well, chalk it up to human nature.

"Sorry, Gwen," she said as she headed downstairs to the kitchen to pop a frozen pizza into the microwave. "This time you're wrong."

She touched the heavy onyx ring that hung suspended from a chain around her neck.

Something else kept her from following her heart out to Nevada where Tom Sagan waited. Something else held her in place when she longed to run free.

And as soon as she figured out what it was, she'd be on the first plane bound for the bright lights of Las Vegas and the man she loved.

That is, if it wasn't too late.

* * *

It was a few minutes after one in the afternoon and the boss was on the warpath.

"What the hell are you waiting for?" Tom glared at the workers seated in the dining hall of the Sagan Fireworks compound. "Lunch hour's over, people. Get off your butts. If you don't give a damn about the contest, say so now and let me find someone who does."

The workers cleared out faster than school kids after the last bell.

"You're a wonderful boss, Son," his mother, Maycee, said, popping up next to him. "That understanding manner of yours should win their undying loyalty."

"I don't give a damn about their loyalty," he said, grabbing a sandwich off the buffet table. "I just want production." He looked at his mother, who was wearing her usual denim shirt and red slacks. "You should understand that."

"And you should understand that loyalty is more important in this business than efficiency. I don't have to tell you how Buck felt about that."

She was right, even though Tom hated to admit the fact. As in any close-knit group whose members depended upon one another for their own survival, the loyalty of the workers in a fireworks compound was vital. Eight hours a day they handled explosives powerful enough to blast them all from Las Vegas to Los Angeles; one moment of anger or carelessness, and all their work, all their effort, could end in disaster.

Buck had taken the utmost care in hiring employees one by one, making sure personalities and egos meshed as smoothly as the chemicals needed to create the fireworks themselves.

Volatile chemicals and volatile personalities were a formula for instant catastrophe.

"I haven't been sleeping," he said finally. "I guess it's beginning to show."

"Anything I can do?"

"Not unless you can show me how to be in two places at once."

They stepped outside into the savage desert sun and walked slowly back toward the main building that housed the offices.

"Why don't you call her?" Maycee shielded her eyes against the glare as she looked up at her son. "You know you want to."

Molly had made sure Tom's romantic entanglement was common knowledge before he was back twenty-four hours. He wasn't secretive by nature, but this ensemble nagging was getting under his skin.

"I've done what I can," he said, holding the door open for his mother. "Right now, I have to concentrate on preparing for the contest."

"And what about after the contest?" she asked, touching his arm. "What then, honey? Will you go to her?"

He leaned against the desk. A few days ago he would have said yes. Now, however, the silence from Boston seemed to grow louder every minute, and his confidence that things would work out was quickly fading.

"I don't know," he said finally. "I don't know what I'm going to do."

Maycee glanced at her enormous watch, and he could see the tug between her need to keep on her writing schedule and her maternal duties.

How well he understood the conflict between responsibility and love. He'd been battling that same conflict every second since he'd left Katie standing in the middle of Logan Airport.

"Buck and Paula would be so proud that you've managed to rebuild and to enter the contest so soon after the accident. But, honey, don't go thinking you've got to win in order to make the honor any more real than it already is." She put an arm around him and gave him a fierce hug. "We've already won as far as I'm concerned. We're carrying on."

Before he could say anything, Maycee—shirttails flapping behind her in a flurry of motion and Chanel No 5—raced off down the hallway toward her workroom.

It was a good thing his mother didn't turn around to impart one last bit of advice, because he was having one hell of a hard time choking back his tears.

He'd been living at the edge of his emotions since he'd come back from his trip. He was short-tempered one moment and highly sentimental the next; his constant mood changes kept everyone at the compound walking on eggshells.

For the last six months he'd eaten, breathed, dreamed the contest. Its significance had gone way beyond the professional; it had become a symbol of all the love he'd felt for his father and fiancée, a way to assuage the guilt he'd carried with him since the night he saw them killed.

In all this time, nothing and no one had been able to break his concentration.

Nothing until Katie Powers.

Now here he was with the contest less than ten days away, and his mind was back in a beach house on Cape Cod with a woman whose passionate, loving nature was trapped behind a wall of sadness that he hadn't had the time or the courage to scale.

Many of the things she'd said at the airport had been right on the mark. Although he'd taken it for granted, his life had been touched by a kind of magic. He'd been given a gift of inner happiness the same way he'd been given physical strength.

He'd never known true guilt or conflict until he'd seen his father and his beloved die before his eyes, leaving him to wonder why he hadn't died with them.

Buck had been planning for this international competition for months before his death.

Now it was up to Tom to see his plans through.

That trip to Japan had been the last step in creating a fireworks spectacular that would rival the handiwork of the gods. Tom wanted to do more with the night sky than they had ever dreamed of.

The four days he'd spent in Boston had been a luxury he shouldn't have allowed himself. But the power of love had been stronger than a thousand rockets, more exciting than a sky filled with a hundred soaring comets.

"Hey, boss. You busy?"

Tom looked up to see Ed McTavitt standing by the door.

Good going, Sagan, he thought, noting the cautious look in the older man's eyes. *Now even your own friends can't stand you.*

"What is it, Ed?"

"Building C's having trouble setting up the cross-match. The way it's going, the shell's gonna pop right over the crowd."

"Damn it to hell." Tom dragged his hand through his hair, pushing it off his forehead. "Did they put the quick-burning fuse inside *and* outside the shell?"

"They followed standard procedure, boss. It still ain't working."

Tom's own fuse was burning pretty quickly itself. "Why didn't Benny come in and tell me himself?"

The look on Ed's face told him all he needed to know.

"Don't answer that, Ed. I've been acting like a real S.O.B., haven't I?"

Ed's weathered face broke into a grin. "Well, now that you mention it, boss, they have been calling you that since you been back."

"And worse?"

"I ain't telling," Ed said with a shake of his head. "Ed McTavitt don't rat on his friends."

The two men laughed and Tom led the way across the compound to Building C.

Maybe he couldn't knock down walls, but at least he could try and mend a few fences.

Robert Morrisson was pacing up and down in front of the restaurant when Katie finally got there. He looked tanned and fit and more than a little worried.

"It's twenty after twelve," he said as he held the door for her. "Where in hell have you been?"

Katie, panting from her race down Beacon Street, leaned against the wall for a second to catch her breath. "I lost track of time."

Robert stared at her as if she'd just declared herself legally insane. "You lost track of time?"

She smoothed down her hair and straightened the collar of her pale linen jacket. "Guilty. I was working on a free-lance job and before I knew it, it was noon. I ran all the way here."

"Jameson's been watching the clock. I told him I'd call you."

She smiled at Robert. "Don't worry. I'll apologize to him."

"I'm not worried about me," he said, guiding her to the table in the main dining room. "I hate to see you start off on the wrong foot with him. He's a tough old— Here she is, Douglas."

Douglas Jameson, tall, elegant and greyhound-slim, rose from his chair to shake Katie's hand. He was every inch the Boston Brahmin. She had no doubt her tardiness had cost her points.

"Ms. Powers."

"Mr. Jameson." She took her seat. "Thank you for delaying lunch."

"Difficulties in traffic, I presume?" Jameson motioned for the waiter.

She started to tell the truth, but the look on Bob's face pulled her up short.

"Boston is horrendous around noontime, isn't it?" she said instead. "One day they'll come to their senses at City Hall and ban cars entirely."

That was music to Jameson's conservative ears. He immediately launched into a speech on the economic and social advisability of such a notion. Robert's eyes glazed over and Katie smiled into her white wine.

She knew exactly what her answer was going to be.

"Damn shame, Katie. A damn shame." Douglas Jameson showed no signs of climbing into the limousine parked at the curb. "We could use someone like you. Innovative thinking. That's what builds nations."

"Well, as I said before, Douglas, I'd be happy to freelance for B, J and C anytime."

"If that's all we can get, I'll take you up on that, Katie. But if you ever want a real chance to get ahead, sign up with us."

Katie looked over at Bob, who was obviously having difficulty keeping a straight face.

"I'll keep that in mind."

"Mr. Jameson, your plane leaves in forty-five minutes." His chauffeur had been waiting patiently with the door open since they came out of the restaurant.

"I'm on my way, Floyd. Damn these cars anyway. Should ban them entirely. Much better idea."

Robert let out a long whistle as the stretch Lincoln pulled away from the curb.

"I don't believe it. You turn down Jameson's best offer in years, and he ends up eating out of your hand. Is it done with mirrors?"

Katie's laugh bubbled over. "I wish I knew. If I did, I could give Lee Iacocca a run for his money."

"If you have the time, why don't we walk over to the Common? I don't have to get back to the office for a while." Bob tugged at his tie in the way she remembered so well. "It's been a long time since we talked."

"I'd like that."

Gwen's comment about unfinished business popped into Katie's mind, but she pushed it aside.

They talked about business and finance and the real estate market in Cambridge as they strolled through the crowded park on their way to the swan boats. Perfectly normal, perfectly ordinary. A conversation much like those they'd had during their marriage.

A conversation careful to avoid any and all painful topics.

This time, however, it wasn't quite enough. The notion of unfinished business had taken hold and wouldn't let her go.

"I never thought I'd see you without a watch, Kate," Bob said as they found a bench beneath an enormous oak tree. "You're changing."

She gestured toward the mustache he'd grown since she last saw him. "So are you, friend. Sunny's influence?"

He grinned and touched the new growth of hair. "Afraid so. She's made a new man out of me."

"The old man wasn't so bad, but I must say, you look extremely happy."

"I am, Kate. I didn't know I had this capacity for happiness."

"How well I know." She hadn't realized how much joy she was capable of until the day she met Tom Sagan. "How is she? Did the second store open on time?"

"Sunny's terrific, and no, it didn't. She didn't like the wallpaper and delayed the opening another two weeks." Bob shook his head. "How she manages to operate at a profit astounds me. She breaks every rule of good business and still cleans up."

"Don't question it, Bob," Katie said, watching a father and son toss a Frisbee across the lawn. She took a deep breath, then asked, "How's Sophie?"

"Fantastic!" Katie had never seen such pure joy on anyone's face before. "Do you know that when I drop into the store to see them, Sophie—" He stopped. A hundred different emotions passed over his face.

"It's all right." Katie let the pain wash over her, then recede. "I'm happy for you."

He took her hand in his. "I don't think Miss Manners covers anything like this, do you?"

"She should. It might have gotten us through some rough patches along the way."

"I love Sophie," he said carefully, "but that doesn't mean I've forgotten Jill."

The instinct to back away from pain resurfaced but, for the first time, Katie pressed on. "For so long I tried to forget her, but now there are times when I have to really work at remembering how red her hair was, how blue her eyes—" Her voice caught, then failed her.

Bob squeezed her hand. "The way she always laughed when we gave her a bath."

The pain tightened itself around her heart.

"There are times when I think I imagined the whole thing, that someone will wave a magic wand and bring her back. Something that terrible shouldn't have happened. We didn't deserve it."

Jill didn't deserve it.

"Don't look for any meaning in it, Kate, because there isn't any. I spent a year tearing myself inside out, trying to figure out how I'd failed, and it still couldn't bring our girl back."

How well Katie understood.

For months she had blamed that glass of wine in her second month, that bike trip in her fourth. Too much exercise. Too little sleep. Every transgression, both real and imagined, pointed toward her guilt and her guilt alone.

Katie had embraced her sorrow with almost selfish intensity, wrapping it around her heart like a shield, certain her pain was greater than anyone else's.

Just because Bob got up each morning and went to work and functioned in a productive fashion, she'd made the supremely arrogant assumption that he'd bounced back from sorrow.

She'd had no idea that her ex-husband had been suffering the same as she.

It hadn't occurred to her to ask.

This raw pain, however, was new and fresh. She had no defenses ready against it. A sob ripped at her throat and she fought it down, but the battle was over before it began.

While she loved Thomas Sagan with all her heart, the arms around her then were the arms she needed. These tears belonged to the daughter she and Robert had created.

These tears belonged to the dreams they'd dreamed as children, only to find the real world a vastly different place.

To her amazement, he held her close and she felt his tears warm against the side of her neck.

Robert Morrisson and Katie Powers finally did what they should have done three years ago: They grieved for their daughter.

"Now here is one of the big advantages of working at home," Katie said half an hour later as she handed Bob a Kleenex. "I don't have to explain my red eyes to anyone."

Bob, amazingly unperturbed at showing private emotion in such a public fashion, blew his nose. "Neither do I," he said, smiling at her. "I'm going home."

"You never looked this happy when we were married," she said, with a rueful shake of her head.

He ruffled her hair. "Neither did you." They stood up and headed off across the Common once again. "You've found someone, haven't you, Kate?"

"Is it that obvious?"

"Only to someone who cares."

She told him a little about Tom. "In a way he reminds me of Sunny," she said as they stopped to buy some ice cream from a vendor. "One of life's lucky ones."

"Sunny will get a kick out of that description."

"Why?" Katie asked as they walked toward the gardens. "It's true, isn't it?"

"Sunny's lucky, all right," he said. "She's lucky she's alive."

He told her the most amazing story about Sunny and a childhood filled with a degree of poverty and brutality that Katie found hard to believe existed in a civilized city like Boston.

She had looked at Sunny, seen a beautiful and happy woman, and assumed that what she saw was all there was to the story.

"Everything she's accomplished, she's accomplished the hard way." The look of admiration and love on Bob's face was almost painful to see. "And she's somehow managed to keep this sense of joy that she brings to everything she touches."

Katie understood his words on the deepest level possible, and for the first time, she saw that the death of their daughter had only hastened the inevitable.

"That's the difference, isn't it?" she asked. "We were too alike, too worried about the same things, too preoccupied with the future to enjoy the present." How could she have missed such a simple truth? "We never made each other laugh."

"He does?" Bob asked, referring to Tom.

"Yes. He makes me happy."

Bob draped an arm across her shoulders as they headed out of the Common.

"Then let me ask you something, Kate." He stopped and looked her straight in the eye. "What the hell are you doing in Boston?"

Laughter rose up from deep inside her, and the last remnant of sorrow disappeared.

"You know what?" she asked, stepping into the street to hail a cab. "I was just asking myself the same question."

A battered taxi screeched to a halt in front of her, and just before she climbed inside, she turned to Bob once more.

"Give Sophie a kiss for me, okay?"

His smile was brighter than she'd ever seen it. "On one condition," he said as he gave her a hug. "Will you send me a postcard from Las Vegas?"

"What makes you think I'll be going to Las Vegas?"

"Because we're so much alike, Katie. Neither one of us is about to let a second chance slip away without a fight."

His words stayed with her the rest of the night.

11

The door slammed shut behind the cleaning service crew the next afternoon, and Katie found herself alone in a silent—but spotless—house.

For the last six hours, the wizards from Now You Can Eat Off the Floor had scrubbed and polished every square inch of Katie's beautifully preserved house, until her nostrils quivered from the smell of Mr. Clean and floor wax.

Radios had blared from odd corners of little-used rooms. Laughter echoed from the basement to the attic.

They'd even left an enormous pot of chili simmering on the back burner of her stove.

The silence now that they'd gone was so overwhelming that she was tempted to mash cracker crumbs into the plush carpet and spill a bottle of ink on the shiny kitchen floor just to have an excuse to call them back in.

As it was, it would be another month before that mausoleum Katie called home would be so lively again.

Not a cheerful thought.

She helped herself to a bowl of chili, then wandered into the pristine living room and clicked on the television. A retired Patriots linebacker was giving the sports update, and she curled up on the couch with her supper and listened halfheartedly.

Maybe she'd go to sleep early. She hadn't slept well at all the night before. Gwen had called as promised, long after midnight, for an update on Katie's lunch meeting with Robert, and the conversation had left Katie feeling unsettled and dissatisfied, with no readily understood reason for either emotion.

The ex-jock rambled on about the Red Sox and life without Yastrzemski, and she looked around for the remote control. She'd rather watch a *Taxi* rerun for the fifteenth time than listen to this constant reverence for past glory.

She fumbled around on the end table and beneath the sofa cushions.

Damn it!

Each time they came in and cleaned, it took a day and a half until she could figure out where everything was. She put her bowl of chili down on the rosewood table in front of the couch and got up to change the station manually, when something caught her interest.

Fireworks.

Spinning comets and shooting stars and spiraling Saturn rings filled her screen with bursts of gold and silver and red.

She sat down on the edge of the table as the bored sports reporter read his copy.

"They held the annual Summer Ladies' Night at Fenway yesterday, capped off by a spectacular fireworks show staged by the Gruccis of Long Island. Crowds at Ladies' Night were estimated to be—"

She jumped up and switched off her set. Her heart pounded with quick, fierce determination.

What on earth was she doing in Boston?

Last night she might have been able to turn a deaf ear to some of her sister's more outlandish statements.

Tonight she wouldn't even try.

Everything Gwen had said last night had been painfully on target.

She was a housewife, that's what she was. A woman well and truly wedded to a house, a pile of wood and bricks and plaster that had a pedigree even longer than her own.

Single-handedly she was upholding a family tradition that not even her own family gave a damn about any longer.

Gwen had followed her heart across the Pacific.

Even her parents, whose roots were deeply embedded in Boston soil, had migrated south in search of sun and surf.

Only Katie remained in Boston, and she didn't like the city any more than Tom did. She was as free as the breeze. Nothing held her down except the ties she allowed to bind her.

Why wait for him to come back to her? Why not pack a bag and fly to Las Vegas first thing in the morning?

He had to be there. With the international competition less than a week away, he could be nowhere else.

She touched the heavy onyx and gold ring now on her middle finger. A wad of tape on the back adjusted the size and made her remember high school and going steady.

Well, this wasn't high school, and she wasn't going steady. And no one said a woman had to sit back and wait for Prince Charming to swoop down and carry her off to the castle in the clouds.

Tom Sagan had made a promise when he gave her the ring, and she was about to show up on his doorstep to collect.

"...three...two...one...hit it!"

Tom watched quietly as the desert sky exploded with color. Next to him, his mother and Molly whistled and clapped as the fiery weeping willow hung overhead, then fell toward earth, its rich amber afterglow outlining the delicate branches of the imaginary tree.

"Great going, boss," Ed said as they waited for the next trial shot to be positioned. "That one alone's worth the price of a ticket to Japan."

Tom had fashioned his willow along the lines of the Japanese *kamuro* shell, the most beautiful of its type. "We have to add more charcoal to the stars," he said. "We need more burning time so it doesn't break that low."

Ed scribbled something in a spiral notepad. "Ain't nothing wrong with what I just saw," the man grumbled.

Tom knew he was pushing them all to the breaking point, but his obsession knew no bounds. It was Sunday night, and the competition was less than a week away. Work, hard and ceaseless, was the only thing that could keep him from spending his days—as well as his nights—thinking of Katie Powers.

"Okay," he yelled to his crew, who sere setting off the fireworks by hand that night. "Send up the blue comet."

A muscle in his jaw began to twitch and he took a deep breath. Blue was going to make him or break him. If he could just stumble upon the right mixture of copper and salts and chlorine, the contest would be his.

But blues were dangerous, the mixture highly unstable. The trick of capturing the exact cobalt color of Katie's eyes still eluded him.

The irony of the situation did not.

The comet shell got good height, and the crackle effect ripped through the sky.

"Looks good," Molly said as the color blossomed. "I think we've got something, Tom."

Tom, however, cursed under his breath. "Too much green. It lacks depth."

"Get your eyes checked." His mother turned to him. "That was superb."

"I know what I'm looking for, damn it!" He exploded like the shells overhead. "That's not even close."

Even Ed, brave and foolish, ventured an opinion. "Boss, I never saw a blue that good. We got it in the bag with that formula."

Tom started to say something but Molly stepped in.

"Come back to the house with me," she said, pulling him toward her Blazer, parked a few hundred feet away. "We'll go through all my paints. Maybe you can show me the color you're looking for."

The hell he could.

Nothing Molly could show him would even come close to the blue of Katie's eyes.

He stopped abruptly a few yards before the truck. "I'm staying out here. I'll go back to the compound and work on the formula for a while."

Molly's response was earthy and unladylike. "The hell with the stupid formula. Will you call her, for God's sake? You're making everyone around here miserable."

How well he knew.

What his sister and mother and everyone else didn't realize was that he was making himself just as miserable. Lady Luck, once his ally, had turned the tables and dealt him a hand impossible to win.

How did you bare your heart to a woman who refused to see past the boundaries of her own?

How did you show your vulnerability when you'd spent most of your life thinking yourself invulnerable?

He'd rather face a line of ancient Grecian fire with its whirlwind of flame and heat than admit that maybe, just maybe, there was no hope for them, after all.

Maybe if she'd been able to get a flight out on Sunday, she wouldn't have had time to get nervous, but Fate had other plans in mind.

There were no seats on Sunday.

Monday, Logan was socked in with the worst electrical storm in thirty-seven years.

Tuesday's flights were filled with Monday's holdovers. Wednesday's were filled with Tuesday's reservations.

By the time she caught a plane early Thursday morning, Katie was a tangled, panicked mass of insecurity.

She thumbed through eight magazines.

She drank four cups of coffee and used the lavatory three times.

She stopped the flight attendant for the sixth time in thirty-five minutes. "When are we supposed to land?"

"Nine a.m., local time." The young woman looked at Katie closely. "Do you need hotel reservations or something, miss?"

Good grief. She hadn't even thought that far ahead. "No—I mean, yes. I don't know."

Superior training kept the attendant from wringing Katie's neck. "If you do, there will be a representative from the chamber of commerce meeting our flight. He'll be able to help you. There's a contest of some sort in town this week; rooms are at a premium."

Great going, Katie thought. At least when Tom showed up at her doorstep unannounced, he'd had the good grace to leave his suitcase at his hotel.

Katie Powers, with her pedigreed Boston background, was going to show up with her matched set of Louis Vuitton under her arm and egg on her face.

She might have lost her heart in Hakone, but right now, she was losing her nerve.

Thursday afternoon, the floor of Molly Sagan O'Reilly's office was littered with sketches for the finale of the competition just thirty-six hours away. Page after page of brilliant ideas—if she did say so herself—all down the drain because Tom Sagan was losing his mind.

Leave it to her brother to wait until the next-to-the-last minute to decide to revamp the whole damned thing. He had burst into her kitchen that morning just as she and Hugh were finishing breakfast, looking for all the world as if he'd spent the night wrestling with a cactus plant.

"Good grief!" She had held a paper napkin in front of her son's eyes. "Don't look, Charlie," she said to the baby, who sat in the high chair amusing himself with strained bananas. "I don't want you to take after your uncle."

Hugh pulled the napkin out of her hands and motioned for Tom to sit down. "Charlie already has Tom's table manners. I don't think further exposure can hurt either one of them."

Tom poured himself a cup of steaming black coffee and grabbed for a slice of wheat toast.

"At least I don't eat strained bananas with my fingers." He tickled his nephew's chubby feet.

"That's about the only bad habit you don't have," Molly said. "You still haven't slept, have you?"

"I'm okay. There's a lot to do."

"It won't amount to much if they have to drag you off to LVMC because you collapsed from exhaustion."

For the first time, Tom didn't meet her eyes. "That's my problem, Mol."

"Call her, Tom."

"Call who?" Hugh asked.

"His Bostonian redhead."

"Her name is Katie."

Molly suppressed a smile. It was even more serious than she had thought.

"I thought you went to Japan." Hugh scooped Charlie up out of his high chair and slung him across his broad shoulders. "How'd you end up in Boston?"

"It's a long story." Tom glared at Molly, who simply smiled at him.

"Let me in on the secret," Hugh said.

Molly kissed the baby, then her husband. "I'll tell you later."

Hugh took Charlie upstairs.

"See what a wonderful sister I am?" Molly said. "I didn't even tell my own husband about her."

"You managed to tell everyone else." He gulped down some coffee. "I didn't come here to talk about my love life."

"What love life? If you can manage one with the woman of your dreams on the other side of the continent, you're more inventive than I thought."

"Mind your own business, Mol."

"I've never known you to be so stubborn. If you love her, call her."

"It's not that simple."

"Then explain it to me."

"Ease up on me, will you?" He dragged a hand through his tangled hair, and her heart suddenly went out to him. "I'm too tired to fight."

"Why don't you go home and get some sleep? You've been up for forty-eight hours."

"Fifty-three, not that I'm counting."

"What good will you be if you fall asleep over the firing board tomorrow night?"

"I won't be at the board," he said. "I'll be on the barge." He polished off his coffee and grabbed another piece of toast. "By the way, I need a new finale."

"You're joking." The finale they'd decided upon had taken her three days to work out. Tom had been unbelievably picky when it came to her choice of blue for a wheel of comets that were supposed to spin off from a waterfall. "I thought it was perfect."

"Not dramatic enough. I want more blue in the first part."

She poured herself some coffee and wiped a smear of strained banana from the tabletop. "What is this obsession with blue anyway? I can give you the most perfect cobalt blue imaginable, but if you can't duplicate it, what's the point?"

His jaw tightened in the same way their father's used to. "I'll duplicate it."

"Then duplicate it in the finale we agreed on."

"We can do better."

"No, Tom. I can't."

They'd set off a trial version that Ed and some of the other old-timers had said was the best they'd ever seen—high praise from men of few syllables. Molly had exhausted every trick of color and balance at her artistic command—there was nothing to improve upon.

"Damn it, Molly!" He dragged his hand through his hair. "You're our ace in the hole. We need your sketches to work from."

"That's it, big brother. If family loyalty doesn't work, try flattery."

"You'll do it?"

"Grudgingly." It was hard to refuse a man who hadn't slept in fifty-three hours and was so lovesick he couldn't see straight. "I have one condition, however."

"You want me to watch Charlie so you and Hugh can go to Hawaii."

She laughed out loud. "Don't tempt me." She got up and hugged him, taking a long, close look at the deep circles under his eyes. "Will you go home and get some sleep?"

So, now, here Molly was five hours later, up to her eyeballs in cobalt blue, trying to come up with an idea that would please her obsessive, maniacally driven brother, whose search for the phantom perfect blue was turning into the search for the Holy Grail.

For the hundredth time she rinsed off her fine-point sable brush in a cup of clear water, then picked up some of the pure cobalt tint on her palette. She was about to sketch in a new swirl of Saturn rings when Ed rapped on the door.

"We got company outside."

She put the brush down. The location of the fireworks compound was not common knowledge. Visitors were discouraged because of the volatile nature of the work done there.

"A reporter?"

Ed shook his head. "Don't think so. She's askin' for Tommy."

Molly wiped her hands on her paint-smeared jeans. "Did you ask for some ID?" Since the unsolved explosion at the Gruccis' compound on Long Island a few years ago, everyone in the pyrotechnics industry had become fanatic about security.

"Sure thing."

He handed Molly an out-of-state driver's license, and she stared at the photo of a beautiful red-haired woman.

Kaitlin Powers of Boston, Massachusetts, had blue eyes.

Pure, deep *cobalt* blue.

The blue Tom had been searching for.

Life, it seemed, was about to get very interesting.

She was Tom's sister, all right. There was no mistaking the blond hair, the golden eyes or the amazingly direct manner.

"You two are making our lives miserable," Molly Sagan O'Reilly said after they shook hands. "I was about to lasso my brother and ship him back to Boston C.O.D."

Katie's mouth dropped open. "You know about Tom and me?"

Molly laughed. "Not as much as I'd like. He's been too damned stingy with the details, if you ask me, but I've been able to fill in the blanks."

God forbid.

"Is he in?" Katie tried to ignore the curious looks from Ed McTavitt and the other men who'd joined him in the doorway to Molly's office. What a romantic reunion this would be.

Any confidence she'd been able to manufacture on the drive from Caesar's Palace to the fireworks compound was rapidly fading away.

"You think we'd be standing here shooting the breeze with you if he was in?" Ed asked.

The younger man next to him laughed. "You could hear the whip cracking all the way across the compound."

She turned to Molly. "Are they talking about the Tom Sagan I know?"

"My brother, the slave driver. He's been eating, breathing and sleeping this damned competition."

Tom a slave driver? Easygoing, happy-go-lucky Tom Sagan? Katie had imagined working for Sagan Fireworks to be a perpetual party.

Molly, however, seemed to think otherwise.

"Look at these," she said, pointing to the dozens of sketches scattered on the floor of her office. "Thirty-seven designs for the finale and not one of them is good enough for that—" Molly caught herself. "Not exactly what you want to hear about your boyfriend, is it?"

Not exactly.

Katie wanted to turn and bolt for the door.

Talking to Gwen about Tom was one thing; being talked about to Molly was another.

Why on earth had she imagined Tom as being so singularly free of family despite the fact that he ran a family business?

A fourth man joined Ed and the other two in the doorway.

"Who's that?" the new arrival asked Ed.

"Tommy's girlfriend."

"The one he found in Japan?"

"Yep."

The new arrival blatantly looked Katie over.

"Do I meet with your approval?" she snapped.

"Honey, if the boss ever gets on your nerves, you just remember old Bobby Squires has the best set of—"

"Bobby!" Molly's voice was stern. "You're married."

"Don't bother me none," he said with a wicked smile, "if it don't bother her."

Katie was hard put to stifle a chuckle. "It bothers me."

The man shrugged good-naturedly. "You win some, you lose some."

"Ignore them," Molly said, turning back to Katie. "We're just one big, rowdy family around here. No secrets."

Katie swallowed hard around her New England reticence. They already seemed to know more than they should. "Not even a few?"

"Well, maybe one or two."

"Is Tom's whereabouts one of them?"

"Hell, no. I sent him home to get some sleep." Molly explained how he'd been working for almost three days straight and had become even more impossible to deal with. "I'll drive you out there, if you have the guts to deal with Il Duce."

She had the guts to deal with him, but not in front of a crowd. "I have a rental car out front. If you'd just give me the address . . ."

"Imagine sending someone out to Tommy's without a guide?" Ed said, sending his cohorts into gales of laughter.

"The land is flat," Katie retorted. "A redwood house should be a pretty easy thing to find."

"How long have you been in town?" Molly asked.

Katie looked at her brand-new Swatch. "About four hours."

"I'll drive you up."

"Draw me a map."

"You'll never find it. Trust me."

Katie turned away from the men in the doorway. "Tom doesn't know I'm here," she said quietly. "I'd feel funny if we—"

"Say no more." Molly turned toward the men who were openly eavesdropping. "Listen, guys. Katie wants to surprise Tom, so don't go shooting off your mouths to everyone in sight. Let's give love a chance."

Katie groaned and covered her eyes. She might as well have hired the Goodyear Blimp to drop fliers announcing her arrival.

She followed Tom's sister through the hallway and out the back door to the parking lot.

Ed and company trailed right behind her. She thought she overheard a fifty-dollar bet going down between Ed and Bobby Squires, but she wasn't about to ask for details.

Molly stopped in front of Katie's rented Chevy.

"You're coming with me?" This was getting more bizarre by the second.

"How else can we talk?" Molly tossed her car keys to Ed. "Follow us out to Tom's, so I can have a ride back." She grinned at Katie. "Something tells me my brother will be too busy to give me a lift."

Katie had to laugh. "You're as pushy as Tom said you were."

"Then we're even, because you're just as stubborn."

Katie opened the car door and motioned Molly inside.

"Hop in," she said. "I think this is the beginning of a beautiful friendship."

Katie waited until the truck with Molly and the four men squashed inside veered off down the road before she knocked on Tom's massive front door. Rejection would be bad enough, but rejection with Ed and company watching as spellbound as if they were at the drive-in was something she couldn't handle.

She knocked at the door.

No answer.

She rang the bell.

Still no answer.

The Jaguar Molly said belonged to Tom was parked in the driveway, so he had to be home. She peeked into the window to the left of the door, but all she could make out was an expanse of hallway with a pale red terra-cotta floor.

She fiddled with the car keys to the rented Chevy, tempted to follow Molly's tire tracks all the way back to the main road.

Then she heard a splashing sound from the rear of the house, followed by a deep bark from a dog that sounded to be the size of a baby *Tyrannosaurus rex*.

This was no time for cowardice. She squared her shoulders, then followed the stone path around the side of the house.

Don't panic. He came halfway around the world for you. This is the least you can do for him.

She prayed that the look on his face would match the emotions in her heart.

The creaking of the gate and Coffee's warning bark alerted Tom that someone had entered the yard.

He had just finished swimming his thirtieth lap and his mind was reluctant to give up the seductive rhythm of the water. He grabbed hold of the edge of the pool and shook his wet hair off his face. Harsh midday sun slanted directly into his eyes, and he squinted toward the spot where Coffee danced attendance on someone standing in the shade of the house. For a moment he thought he saw the shimmer of red hair, but that was a trick of the desert light. A mirage brought on by nights of wishful thinking.

"Can I help you?" he called out as he hoisted himself from the pool and reached for a towel.

"Yes," a familiar voice said from the shadows. "You can tell me you're happy to see me."

For one terrible moment he wasn't entirely sure that he was.

12

When Tom raised his long, bronzed body out of the pool and walked toward her with his muscles glistening in the sun, desire did more to raise her temperature than the desert heat.

It wasn't until he came closer that she saw the toll his obsession with winning the competition had taken on him. A two-day stubble might have done wonders for Don Johnson's popularity, but it made Tom's handsome face look haggard. Dark circles rimmed his amber eyes and faint lines circled his mouth.

He was still an incredibly handsome man, but those golden-boy looks had subtly shifted, revealing an intensity she hadn't suspected.

He was the man she loved.

He was a stranger.

She stepped out of the shadow of the house.

"If you don't tell me you're happy to see me sometime in the next ten seconds, I'm going to slink down the driveway and go back to the airport."

"The hell you will."

He pulled her against him. Her body sizzled against his cool wet flesh. His large hands cradled her skull as he bent down to crush her mouth with his. The sensations of cold where she was hot, of wet where she was dry, were erotic in the extreme.

He took her breath away with the force of his kiss, and she pulled back in order to recover her equilibrium. She drew in a gulp of dry, hot desert air while he pressed moist kisses along the side of her throat.

"You're glad to see me?" she managed. A foolish question when he was igniting brushfires everywhere he touched, but she was beyond logic and reason.

The prim and proper Brooks Brothers shirt fell open to her waist. Even the sun on her bare flesh couldn't compare to the fierce heat of desire. Her arms were trapped by the shirt and she was helpless as he stared at her exposed breasts.

He pulled her against his wet and hard body; her nipples tightened in response to the feel of his cool skin against hers. He plunged one hand deep into her thick red hair and brought her mouth back to his. His tongue traced the outline of her full lips, then slid between them in a kiss of such overwhelming intensity that she felt dizzy. With his other hand he pulled her shirt out of the waistband of her pants and traced his fingers up her spine, making her tremble violently against him.

There was something undeniably savage in his excitement, something wild and primitive that she hadn't seen before.

He drew his tongue across her breasts and she moaned.

"You're burning."

"I know," she whispered.

He picked her up and carried her toward the house, and she didn't bother to tell him it wasn't the sun that had turned her to flame.

The sight of Katie, half naked and flushed with passion, pushed Tom over the edge into madness.

A ridiculous anger had seized him when he first saw her standing in the shadow of his house, but that anger had quickly been supplanted by a powerful blend of love and lust that drove everything else from his mind for the moment.

All he could see were her cobalt-blue eyes as he placed her on his bed and covered her body with his.

All he could hear were her cries of pleasure as he entered her.

All he could feel was the way her body clung to his, drawing him more deeply inside.

Their coupling was quick and fierce, and colored by a thousand conflicting emotions that he didn't have time to unravel.

He had wanted her to take the next step and reach out to him. She had. The fact that she was in his arms was testimony to that fact.

He should be ecstatic.

He wasn't.

Admit it, he thought as they lay together afterward. *The thought of exposing your real self scares the hell out of you.*

He had wanted her to understand all that he was about, but at his own time, his own pace. She had no business being there. Nothing on earth could have kept him from going back to Boston and claiming her as his own.

She should have waited.

He couldn't afford to be distracted. He couldn't afford a second's loss of concentration. The memory of that other contest, that other night, hovered just beyond reach, reminding him of his failures.

He would have to find a way to send his brave New Englander back home to Boston and hope that she would understand.

Tom looked down at her lovely sleeping face.

He wasn't at all sure that he did.

Those beautiful golden eyes of his were watching her.

Katie buried her face deeper into the pillow and feigned sleep. His gaze moved from her shoulder to her breasts to the length of her arm outside the cover; she knew by the sharp awareness that sliced through her and drew blood.

Something was terribly wrong.

Although they'd made love as if starved for the sight and sound and scent of each other, there'd been a sense of desperation in Tom's fevered kisses, a sense of regret in his caress.

So much for grand gestures.

If only she could blink her eyes and wake up back in her own bed in her own empty house on Beacon Hill. Unfortunately, magic was beyond her grasp at the moment, and she had to figure a way to recoup her losses and make a dignified retreat.

The fact that her heart was breaking was nobody's business but hers.

Finally she opened her eyes.

"Hi," he said, touching her cheek. "Sleep well?"

She nodded. "And you?"

"I didn't."

She touched the dark circles beneath his eyes. "Looks like you haven't for quite a while."

"It's almost over," he said, pushing a wave of hair out of her eyes. "Just one more night."

She was finding it hard to keep her breathing calm and steady as a bizarre blend of pain and desire waged war inside her body.

An uncomfortable silence fell across the bed.

He sat up against the headboard and looked down at her. She knew even before he said it.

"Go home, Katie."

"No, Tom."

Tom stared at this red-haired stranger in front of him. Obviously she'd misunderstood his statement.

"I want you to go home."

"And I said no." She sat up and the sheet slipped down to her waist, but she made no move to cover herself.

He was at a distinct disadvantage.

"I have a dinner to go to tonight, and I'll be working straight through until the contest tomorrow evening."

"I'll invite myself to dinner with you." She flashed his father's ring at him. "We're going steady, remember?"

He scraped his hair off his forehead with the back of his hand. "What about after dinner? I don't have time to baby-sit you."

Those beautiful eyes flashed fire at him. "Las Vegas is a big town, Mr. Sagan, and I'm a grown woman. I'm sure I can find some way to amuse myself."

He looked at her, his bare-breasted beautiful warrior, and groaned. She was a distraction of the most dangerous kind, and he was too close to winning to risk all now.

He got up and pulled a worn pair of jeans out of his closet. "Get dressed. I'll take you to the airport."

She didn't move.

He tugged at the sheet but she held it fast.

"Damn it, Katie. I can't make it any plainer. I love you, but I don't want you here. Not now."

She stood up and faced him toe to toe. "And I don't care what you want, Tom Sagan. I'm here to stay."

"I'll fly to Boston as soon as the contest is over."

"Don't bother. I won't be there."

"You don't understand," he said, pulling on his pants and zipping them. "This is something you can't help me with."

She didn't move a muscle, but he thought he detected a look of defeat in her eyes. He knew he was hurting her, but it couldn't be helped. Two days from now, when it was all over, he would go to her with his heart on his sleeve and ask forgiveness.

For so long he'd been a failure in his own eyes. He couldn't stand to be a failure in hers as well.

"Now get dressed, Katie. I'm putting you on the next plane for Boston."

Suddenly the situation seemed absurd. Standing there stark naked arguing with a fully dressed man was probably the height of poor judgment.

This wasn't the lighthearted, happy man she'd met on that train in Japan. Whoever he was, he'd been a product of moonlight and magic—an illusion like the fireworks, and the notion of love at first sight.

If he wanted her to leave so badly, perhaps she should put her clothes back on and leave while she still had at least a shred of dignity left.

Coward, her heart whispered, *you've found what you've been searching for. Don't let him go without a fight.*

There was more to Tom Sagan than she'd been willing to acknowledge before. He wasn't quite as happy, quite as lucky or quite as uncomplicated as she'd first thought.

She'd fallen in love with one man to find another, more complex, man hidden inside. She'd made the mistake of accepting the obvious with Robert; she had no intention of making that mistake with Tom.

If she left now, she'd never know if what they'd found together on that mountainside in Japan was the real thing or just a memory to savor in her old age.

To hell with memories. She wanted more—much more.

She'd seen him laugh, and now she wasn't afraid to see him cry.

"Last chance, Katie," he said. "Can I take you to the airport?"

"No," she said, meeting his eyes head-on. "I'm staying right here."

She had come to do battle, and it was winner take all.

As they drove back into town that afternoon, Tom thought, *She's a different person.* She looked the same, she sounded the same, she felt the same in his arms, but nothing about this Katie Powers was quite the way he remembered.

That touch of sadness he'd first noticed in Japan had been replaced by a sense of determination that threw him off balance.

In Japan, he'd been the one to make the first move.

In Boston, he'd been the one who set things in motion. Showing up at her doorstep with a bouquet of flowers in his hands and his heart on his sleeve had effectively given him the edge in the relationship.

He'd gambled on her own natural reticence to give him the space and time he needed to take care of unfinished business. What he hadn't gambled on was having his fierce New Englander swoop down on him and call his bluff.

"Make a left on to Las Vegas Boulevard South," he told her at a traffic light. "Caesar's is on the left."

She gave him a quick glance. "I know."

"There isn't a room left in town," he continued. "I thought we would share my suite."

Despite their Vegas base of operations, Sagan Fireworks was going all out for the competition and had booked a floor of the luxurious Caesar's Palace for key employees and their families for the weekend. The Sagan "family" would have a private dinner tonight, followed by the more lavish extravaganza that the contest committee would host tomorrow night just before the contest itself.

"I have my own, thanks."

"How did you manage that? I didn't think even Ron and Nancy could wangle a room this weekend."

"I'm pretty good at fending for myself, Tom." She flashed him a smile, then aimed his own words back in his direction. "I don't need a baby-sitter."

He winced. "That was a stupid remark. I apologize."

"Apology accepted."

She stopped at a traffic light by the Sahara Hotel. The squeals of kids playing on the water slide at Wet & Wild Amusement Park filtered through the closed windows of the air-conditioned car.

He took a deep breath. "This is a tough time for me, Katie." His words came with difficulty, for he was closer to revealing his vulnerabilities than ever before in his life. "Nonstop work, the contest—" He shook his head. "Not exactly the height of romance."

"No, it's not," she said, "but it's a start."

Maybe.

He looked at the face of his beautiful Yankee.

And maybe after she found out about the failures hiding behind the golden-boy facade, she would head back to Boston on the first available plane.

Winning the competition would be small compensation for such a terrible loss.

Ed McTavitt and Molly Sagan O'Reilly were waiting for them in the lobby at Caesar's. Katie couldn't help but notice the curious looks they gave to one another as she and Tom approached them.

Ed spoke first. "Big surprise, huh, boss? Not everyone gets a package like that on his doorstep."

Tom looked down at Katie. "Especially without a forwarding address."

Katie patted her pocketbook where her plane ticket back home was stashed. "Don't worry," she retorted. "Return postage is guaranteed."

Ed turned to Molly. "What the hell are they talkin' about?"

"Beats me," Molly said, "but I think there's trouble in paradise."

Normally Katie would have tried to disappear behind a potted plant at such an open discussion of highly personal matters. Now, however, she took it as a matter of course.

Tom had told everyone about Chapter One.

Now she would fill them in on Chapter Two.

"I don't think Tom's used to having strangers pop up on his doorstep," she said coolly. "The shock may have been too much for him."

"Wait a minute!" Ed scratched his head and turned toward Tom. "Didn't you pop up on her—"

"Let's go." Tom grabbed Ed's sleeve. "I thought you were driving me out to Lake Mead so we can start wiring the rockets."

"I think my brother's trying to change the subject," Molly said.

"You get that feeling, too?" Katie was getting an unholy kick out of his discomfort.

Ed fished the keys to his truck out of his back pocket. "He did pop up on your doorstep in Boston, didn't he, Ms. Powers?"

"Call me Katie," she said, "and yes, he did."

Ed's weather-beaten face split into a wide and wicked smile. "Seems to me, then, turnabout's fair play, boss."

Tom glared at Ed and Molly. "Is this a conspiracy of some kind? I deserve more respect than this."

Molly laughed. "No, you don't."

"I have to take their word for it," Katie said. "They've known you longer."

Tom pulled Katie behind an eighteen-foot replica of Michelangelo's David. "Damn it, Katie!" He took her in his arms and kissed her soundly. "Why the hell couldn't you just wait for me?"

At last—the big question.

"Because I love you too much," she said simply. "Because life is too short to wait for the perfect moment."

Because it was time for her to look beyond herself and into the heart of the man she loved.

"I'm not what you think I am, Katie," he said, his voice fierce with emotion. "You may want to use that return ticket."

"I have it if I need it," she said with a smile. "I'm not afraid to know everything about you."

He said nothing, simply kissed her again, then, with a nod toward Molly, followed Ed out of the hotel.

"How he can look like an angel and act like the devil's own is beyond me," Molly said as the two men disappeared through the archway. "You've got your work cut out for you, Katie."

"It looks that way." She reached up to fix the tortoiseshell pin that held her thick hair off her neck.

Molly grabbed Katie's left hand. "That's Buck's ring."

"Tom gave it to me. Who's Buck?"

Molly's face softened and her eyes filled with tears. "Our dad. Tom hasn't had that ring off his finger since the funeral."

Katie touched the heavy onyx ring. It had been valuable to her before; now it was priceless. "I had no idea."

"I've always wanted a sister." Molly gave Katie a swift hug. "Come on. Let's go wild at Neiman-Marcus. We have to get you sequined and beaded for tomorrow night."

"No sequins and beads tonight?"

"With our rowdy crew? Jeans are more like it." Molly paused. "You *do* wear jeans in Boston, don't you?"

"You're more like your brother than I first thought," Katie said. "Do you have any other questions about Boston that you want to get off your chest?"

Molly's grin was full of mischief. "Tell me, Katie," she said as they headed for the parking lot. "How do you Bostonians feel about baby-sitting?"

* * *

How Katie Powers with her Boston ways and Eastern upbringing had managed to fit right in with his decidedly non-finishing-school family was beyond him. Ed and the other men were obviously smitten with her beauty. She and Hugh had had a forty-five minute discussion on bringing computer technology to the masses. His mother had found another writer who understood the problems inherent in the business, and Molly acted as if Katie were a long-lost sister who'd finally found her way back home.

It was he who felt out of place, as if he'd been dropped into the midst of strangers. Past and future seemed to be tugging at his sleeves, and the present was so filled with thoughts of the contest that he found it impossible to make sense out of anything.

The afternoon out at Lake Mead had been long and hot and filled with tension. Each of the five competing countries were designated a roped-off section of lakeside, and what started off as light banter between rivals had deteriorated to out-and-out warfare by early evening. For once, language barriers had proved no obstacle.

Henri Boudreau, who owned the French team, strolled past the enormous barge Tom and Ed were rigging up to hold the fourteen hundred shells needed for the finale. "They ask for a fireworks show, *mes amis*," he said. "Not a *cataclysme!*"

Tom had made sure that their hired guards would keep their eyes out for Henri until Tom returned after the dinner.

He motioned for the waiter to bring more champagne.

"Enjoy it now, folks," he said as the waiter began refilling their glasses, except for Tom's and Ed's. "Starting tomorrow morning, it's nonstop work."

Ed groaned and buried his grizzled head in his hands. "He doesn't even give us one night to howl." He looked at Maycee, who presided over the other end of the table. "What's with this new generation, anyway, May? Don't they know nothing about fun?"

"Buck was the one who knew about fun, Ed. Tom takes after me: work, work, work."

Katie looked up from her salad. "Did I hear right?"

"I told you he was a slave driver," Molly said, waving her butter knife in his direction. "Nose to the grindstone."

Katie leaned across the table. "I thought you were the original free spirit."

"Don't pay any attention to them," Tom said, shifting in his seat. "I ask them to work one week out of fifty-two, and listen to the flak I have to take."

Ed hooted with laughter.

"If only Buck were here to listen to some of this malarkey!" Bobby Squires, who usually had the market cornered on Coors, reached for his second glass of champagne. "I can still remember back when he'd have to haul Tom's skinny butt back here in the pickup to get him to do any work."

Another man chimed in. "That kid spent more time hitching rides than any hobo I ever met."

Some of the other old-timers began trading stories about Tom and his father. The more outrageous the stories got, the more Katie seemed to enjoy them—and the more uncomfortable Tom became.

"You have a cruel heart, Katie Powers," he said, raising his voice to be heard above the dance music drifting in from the other room. "They give me a hard time, and you laugh about it?"

"I love it." Her bright blue eyes danced with amusement. "I adore finding out all of your deep, dark secrets."

"I have no deep secrets," he said, standing up. "Isn't that what you liked about me?" That illusion had appealed to him, as well.

"I've changed my mind," Katie said. "I've decided you're a man of mysteries, and I mean to unravel each one of them."

He started to say something, when he caught the tail end of a conversation between Maycee and Ed about trouble with a firing switch. If a firing switch went bad, the whole twenty-minute exhibition would be ruined.

"What's that about a firing switch?"

Ed turned to him. "Nothing to get hot and bothered about, boss. Bobby got it working again."

He tried to get his mind back on the dinner, but the thousands of details surrounding tomorrow's exhibition raced through his mind. A fireworks competition was a rare thing indeed in the United States. The stakes were as high as the danger involved.

You either won or you lost. There was no such thing as second place.

He looked over at the ring on Katie's hand, at the outer edge where the gold had melted inward in the heat of the explosion.

How well he knew.

Tom's body was present at the dinner, but it was obvious to Katie that his mind was back on the shores of Lake Mead. The orchestra in the next room began to play between the main course and dessert, and she pushed her chair away from the table and motioned to him.

"Come on." She extended her hand. "We've never danced together."

That started a new round of friendly, if ribald, teasing, which Tom bore with grouchy good grace.

"Ignore them," she said as they walked across the marble floor toward the ballroom. "They're just high-spirited."

"You seem to know them better than I do. Are you sure you've only been here twelve hours?"

"No," she said as she went into his arms. "I feel as if I've been here all my life."

His arms went around her and they began swaying with the music. A tall blonde in a see-through red lace body stocking cha-cha'd by with a skinny man who had a bald spot the shape of Texas.

"That's my hometown," Tom said. "Not exactly Beacon Hill, is it?"

"No," Katie answered. "I love it."

He looked at her. "You're kidding?"

"No, I'm not." She laughed at the expression on his face. "From the second I saw a woman dressed as a gypsy giving out marriage license applications in front of the Little Chapel of the Tumbling Dice, I was hooked."

Tom still looked disbelieving, but it was true. Las Vegas was bold, brassy and undeniably tacky—and she loved it.

In Boston, every building and tree had two hundred years of history attached to it. In Las Vegas, there was only the future.

Boston set boundaries, while Las Vegas urged you to go beyond them.

"You've changed," he said as the band segued into a waltz. "I can't put my finger on it, but something's different."

"Every action has a reaction," she said. "You didn't think you could sweep into my life the way you did and not change things, did you?"

"I never thought that far ahead, sweet Katie. I only knew I had to see you again."

"Poor Tom," she said. "I bet you're wishing you'd been less impulsive."

He held her closer. "No, I'm only wishing I had more time right now. There are many things I'd like to—"

Ed McTavitt popped up next to Tom. "We'd better hit the road, boss. I told the other guys we'd relieve them by eleven."

Tom kissed Katie quickly, fiercely.

"You'll be gone all night?"

"Probably."

She slipped a key into his pocket. "I'm a light sleeper."

He grinned. "I'll be back for breakfast."

They went back into the dining room so he could say good-night to Maycee and Hugh and the others. Katie watched, fascinated, as Maycee hugged Ed and Tom and Molly, who was going out to the site with them, then murmured a quick prayer whose words Katie couldn't quite hear.

"It isn't that dangerous, is it?" she asked Hugh as Maycee walked the others out to the parking lot. For some reason, danger had never occurred to her before. "That was just for luck, wasn't it?"

"In their business, you need it," Hugh said, watching his wife disappear down the corridor. "You can mistreat a chemical nine hundred and ninety-nine times and get away with it, but the thousandth time..."

His words faded in the warm summer air as a chill ran up Katie's spine.

13

To worked through the night and well past dawn before he stopped to rest.

He trusted no one but himself to do the final wiring of the explosives. He would ask no one else to ride the barge that would carry those explosives into the middle of Lake Mead that night.

If things went well, he would have the ultimate satisfaction of proving to himself that he could do it.

If not—at least no one else would ever pay for his mistakes again.

A new guard came on duty and flashed his searchlight at Tom in greeting.

More than anything, he wanted to get into his car and go back to the hotel and take comfort in Katie's arms. He stifled a yawn. Unfortunately, there was work to do, and less than fifteen hours in which to do it. Comfort such as he found with her would have to wait just a little longer.

Ed was curled up nearby, his head resting on a rock, his leather jacket draped over his chest. Tom sat down and leaned against an empty crate.

Maybe if he just closed his eyes for a moment . . .

* * *

Tom knocked on the door of Katie's hotel room a little after six o'clock that evening. He'd been out at the contest site all day. His nerves were stretched as taut as the wires on the firing board; his emotions were ready to pop like the explosives they'd been loading. If he could just hang on a little longer, it would be— Katie opened the door and smiled at him, and for a moment he forgot all.

She was everything beautiful he'd ever tried to create in the night sky, except that she was real and she was here and she was his.

Katie shimmered in a dress of silver and gold that seemed to capture her own radiance and toss it back at the world. With her shiny red hair piled loosely atop her head and those incredible blue eyes that he could never duplicate with any of the magic at his command, she was lovelier than anything he'd dared dream about.

"You didn't have to knock," she said, motioning him inside. "You have the key."

He felt suddenly, absurdly shy. "I left it in my room."

She picked up a small glittery evening purse from the top of her dresser. "I'm ready. I can't wait to see what Mrs. Boudreau is wearing. Molly told me she spends as much on clothes as her husband does on perchlorates."

"Perchlorates?"

Katie laughed and put her room key in her purse. "I've been taking a crash course in pyrotechnics, courtesy of your sister."

She closed the door behind them and they walked down the silent hallway toward the elevator. He couldn't help but wonder what else Molly might have told her.

* * *

Las Vegas was known for its love of excess, but the party in the main ballroom of Caesar's Palace that night was extraordinary even by Las Vegas's standards.

"If only I had the sequin concession in this place, I could retire a millionaire," Katie whispered to Tom as she stood next to him on the receiving line.

"You should see Monte Carlo during their fireworks competition," he said. "Makes this look like a convention of undertakers."

The marble-and-gilt ballroom glittered with stardust and diamonds and an intense buzz of anticipation that heightened the unreality of the entire setting. Although Tom was dressed in a perfectly tailored tux—his curly hair under control for a change—his muscles were coiled tight beneath the civilized suit, and she could sense the restraint necessary for him to endure the pre-dinner formalities.

Tom wasn't the only one feeling the strain: Since spending the day with Maycee at the Sagan compound, Katie's understanding of the complexities of the business had increased, and with it, her uneasiness.

The buildings where the fireworks were assembled were built along the lines of World War II bunkers. Static electricity was such a real and present danger in the dry desert sun that before entering any of the buildings, Katie, like everyone, had to touch a copper plate above the door in order to ground herself. Rubber-soled shoes were a must; long hair was tied back and slicked down; silk underwear—absurd as that sounded—was strictly forbidden.

It was a world unto itself. A world that blended beauty and danger in the most elemental way.

The three judges were a somber group who shook hands with both Katie and Tom in the same formal way they had greeted the representatives from the other four countries involved.

"We're in trouble," Molly said as they took their seats at the first of the Sagan tables. "Did you see the way they smiled at Donatelli's wife? I think the Italians have the edge now."

"I think wearing a dress cut down to her knees had something to do with that smile, Mol," Tom said.

Molly nudged her husband in the ribs and fingered the strap on her shimmering black dress. "What do you think? Should I show a little cleavage?"

Katie smiled as Molly and Hugh started their patented bantering. The atmosphere at the table was so charged that she'd been tempted to stand up and start telling jokes—anything to break the tension.

Tom glanced at his watch. "Come on," he muttered. "We have a hell of a lot to do when we get out to Mead."

Ed McTavitt looked up from his shrimp cocktail. "If it ain't done by now, it ain't ever gonna be done."

Despite the Vegas glamour, the precontest dinner proceeded with European formality. Each of the five countries chosen to compete—England, France, Italy, Japan and the United States—would be introduced alphabetically, and a short film presentation on each would follow.

Katie shifted in her chair and glanced at Tom. He'd never last until the end of the program.

She stifled a very unsophisticated yawn. She wasn't entirely sure she'd last.

* * *

The films had been made by an independent film-maker and they were deadly dull.

The sound of rustling satin and silk almost drowned out the clatter of the knives and forks. If it hadn't been for the excellent dinner to keep her occupied, Katie would have fallen asleep with her head on the center-piece.

Tom and the others were faring no better.

Molly and Hugh left during the Italian presentation so they could check on the baby, and so Molly could change into her work clothes.

A few of the other men were carpooling in the company van for the forty-five-minute drive out to Lake Mead, and they left before the lights in the dining room came up. Maycee was determined to stick it out until the bitter end, as was Katie.

Tom, however, was ready to explode louder than the biggest rocket.

He leaned across the table. "As soon as the intros are over, we're splitting," he said to Ed. "England leads off at eight-thirty. I want as much time as we can to get squared away."

Ed seemed to know arguing was a lost cause, and he just nodded and puffed on his cigarette.

The emcee took the stage. "And now we come to our last contestants: America's preeminent fireworks family, Las Vegas's own Sagan Fireworks, Incorporated."

Maycee and Ed stood up and took their bows, acknowledging the hometown crowd's wild applause. To Katie's surprise, Tom kept his seat.

"Stand up," she said to him. "It's not every day you get a thundering ovation."

He barely seemed to hear her. His concentration was evidently on something else.

"It's been a difficult two years for the Sagan family, as we all know," the emcee continued when the applause died down. "Buck Sagan was the backbone of Sagan Fireworks." More applause. Tom looked down at the table. "But as Buck would have wished, the company he started has continued on with Maycee as its heart, Molly as its artistic inspiration and Tom as its soul and muscle. He would have been proud."

The applause was deafening. Maycee's smile was shaky. Ed wiped his eyes with the back of his hand and sniffed loudly. Only Tom remained impassive.

Katie's apprehension increased.

The lights went down again and the film on the Sagan firm began to roll, following much the same format as the four films before it. An overview of the surrounding area, a bit of history, an introduction to the people in charge. They were about to show a clip from another competition when Tom pushed his chair back.

"Come on, Ed," he said low. "Let's get going."

Ed's eyes were glued to the screen suspended over the stage.

"Let's move it, McTavitt."

No response. The film was a whirl of color and sound, snapping reds, hissing golds, a fiery, sizzling burst of amber and silver. Suddenly Katie realized that the voice narrating the competition clip was Tom's.

A brief shot of him, looking tanned and blond and absolutely gorgeous, sitting next to a broadcaster beneath the Brooklyn Bridge in New York.

"Sagan Fireworks does it again," the broadcaster said. "Another brilliant display!"

The bridge was outlined in a spray of fiery water-falls.

"We're coming up onto the finale now," Tom's voice said over the cheering of the crowd and the snap and report of the fireworks. "You might watch for an enormous bouquet of flowers that—"

On the tape, his voice stopped suddenly. A low rumble was heard. The barge from which the shells had been sent up seemed to generate an endless spray of comets and wheels and a thousand flowers.

Next to her, Tom stood up.

"Fantastic!" the broadcaster's voice screamed over the wild cheering of the crowd. "Fantastic!"

The screen faded to black, followed by a silent message:

> Jimmy "Buck" Sagan 1926-1984
> Paula McTavitt 1956-1984

There was a moment of respectful silence, then the spectators in the ballroom stood up and began to clap, a rising crescendo of tribute to two of their own.

Maycee turned away from the screen and Ed McTavitt put one burly arm around her shoulders. The others at the table were quiet.

Tom sat motionless, his hands gripping the edge of the table. Then he jumped up and disappeared out of the ballroom.

Katie was numb. The idea that death could hide in the midst of such unearthly beauty was a travesty of the magic they tried to create.

The idea that Tom had lost his father in the pursuit of that beauty was obscene.

The idea that she could lose Tom in that same pursuit was terrifying.

She ran out of the ballroom after him.

She found him out by the empty swimming pool. He was standing with his tuxedo jacket slung over his shoulder, shirt collar opened, leaning against a wrought-iron railing.

It was almost dark, and impossible to see the expression in his eyes.

"Are you all right?"

He didn't say anything, just looked out over the enormous pool.

She put her hand on his arm. "I wish you'd told me."

"Why? It wouldn't change anything, would it?"

"You listened to me," she said, thinking about the night at the Cape when she told him about Jill. "I'd like the chance to do the same for you."

"There's nothing to listen to. You just had the whole story spread out in front of you in living color. What more do you need to know?"

She took a deep breath. "Who was Paula?"

He met her eyes. "Ed's daughter."

"And?"

"And the woman I was engaged to marry."

She hadn't even suspected. Now she wondered how she could have been such a fool. No one lived thirty-two years without knowing sorrow.

Not even Tom.

The ring on her finger felt suddenly heavy. "I'm so sorry."

His tie hung loosely around his neck, but he tugged at it as if it were a noose. "I rigged that damned barge,

Katie. I wired every one of those triggers to go off in the set. My fingerprints were all over that son of a bitch."

His anger swirled around them like a violent red cloud. "It was an accident, Tom. Molly told me how even a change in weather can—"

His expletive split the stillness. "You set it up, you ride with it. It's as simple as that."

"You couldn't have changed things," she said softly. "Aren't you the one who believes in Fate and Karma and the lure of Lady Luck? What happened is what was meant to happen."

"I could have changed things, all right, Katie." She had never seen eyes so filled with pain as his. "I could have saved their lives and I saved mine instead." A short laugh tore up from his throat. "You did say I was one of the lucky ones, didn't you?"

A branch crackled and they turned in the direction of footsteps coming up the path.

Ed McTavitt, silhouetted by a small light at the edge of the pool, stopped a few feet away from them. The orange dot of his cigarette glowed eerily against the darkness.

"It's time," Ed said.

Tom pulled Katie into his arms. He didn't kiss her. The intensity of his embrace made her weak with longing and fear.

He released her, then looked at Ed. "Let's get the hell out of here."

She grabbed Ed's arm as he went to follow his boss. How had he managed to welcome her so warmly into their lives when his own loss had been so great?

"I didn't know until tonight," she said quietly. "I'm sorry."

Ed shrugged and she caught the scent of Old Spice and tobacco. "I made my peace with it. That boy did nothing wrong. It's been a long time coming, but I think he's going to learn that tonight."

The soft fragrant night seemed fraught with hidden danger. "I'm scared, Ed."

He patted her on the shoulder. "So am I, darlin'. It's when you stop being scared that you gotta worry."

Ed turned and disappeared down the pathway, and Katie murmured a childhood prayer she'd thought long forgotten.

Tonight they would need all the help they could get.

Ed wouldn't take no for an answer.

"You can't hold me back, boss," he said as Tom entered the boat that would take him out to the barge.

"I'm going to do this alone, Ed." After all that had happened, didn't the man understand the danger? His guilt?

"Now you listen to me, son." Ed's voice was stern, almost paternal. "I got as many guilty feelings as you do. I lost my Paulie and my best pal that night. But if you think I'm gonna sit here while you go out there and take all the glory yourself—well, son, that ain't the way it's gonna be."

Tom knew it wasn't the glory Ed wanted to share; it was the danger. The bond between them was forged in fire.

"Come on, you old coot," Tom said, making room for him in the boat. "You're crazy enough to swim all the way out there."

Ed grinned. "Now you're talkin', boss. I always knew you were a reasonable sort."

Their moment had finally arrived.

And like it or not, Tom was scared.

The image of the golden willow seemed to linger in the air.

"*Tremolante*, the old-timers called it," Molly said, by way of explaining the stardust aftereffect of only the finest shells. "We call it glitter, but it's magic just the same."

Katie watched as the last of the Japanese flowers arced, then faded away.

The applause from the hundreds of spectators on the lakeshore was deafening.

"It's going to be tough, isn't it?" she asked, thinking of the mind-boggling displays of tamed fire she'd seen in the past two hours.

"We have a few things up our sleeves," Molly said, but Katie could hear the apprehension in her voice.

Short of calling on Zeus to wield his magic, there was little Katie could think of that could surpass what she'd just seen.

According to Molly, the English had done exceptionally well. The finale the French had planned broke too low and the effect was diminished. The Italians were bigger on concussion than harmony, a definite problem with these particular judges. The Japanese had, of course, been superb.

Three rockets were sent up from the Sagan barge and the simultaneous reports echoed across the lake.

Molly took both Katie's hand and Hugh's. "Here goes."

The show began slowly, with stars and rockets in different color combinations streaking and tumbling across the night sky. Gold and silver, amber and red—

all blended and spiraled past Katie's eyes accompanied by a constant low rumble of thunder.

As the colors built in intensity, so did the thunder. Its deep roar rattled inside her bones. Her teeth vibrated with it. The sky split open with barrages of silver and white that seared her eyes and pounded against her brain. The smell of gunpowder singed her nostrils.

She had to remind herself that beauty often masked a greater danger.

A line of golden fire shot up from the barge, followed by another, then another, until it seemed impossible to increase the noise level, and she shouted into that noise, carried away by the sheer insanity of it.

The sky was ablaze with golden fire.

Suddenly, it fell quiet. Molly's grip on her hand tightened. Katie swallowed against an unreasonable rush of fear. The barge was dark. There was no sign of movement.

And then, just before the tension grew unbearable, a pair of silvery stars went up, followed by two madly spinning silver Saturn rings. The mighty roar of the explosions was gathered into the hills and then flung back at the crowd of spectators, magnified by the lake a thousand times, until Katie felt part of the sound.

Just as the final barrage of silver shells peaked, one lone shell rose higher than any and opened slowly, a glittering cascade of vibrant, electric blue that made Molly cry out, "My God, that might do it!"

Everyone watched the sky.

Only Katie watched the barge, and when she saw the shadowy outlines of two figures gazing toward the heavens, she touched the heavy ring on her hand and whispered a soft "Thank you."

14

Tom and Ed McTavitt watched as the elusive blue flame trembled, then died.

They didn't say a word. They didn't have to. That perfect cobalt fire—the color of Katie's eyes—said it all.

That's when Tom noticed the silence from the crowd. There hadn't been silence after the other contestants' shows. Sweat trickled down his back.

"They're not doing anything, Ed." He turned back toward the other man. "What's going on?"

And then it started. At first it sounded like the crescendo of noise from their finale reverberating across the lake.

"What the—?"

Ed threw his cap into the air. "That's for us, Tommy!" Ed grabbed him in a bear hug. "That's all for us!"

It wasn't an echo at all. It was the sound of car horns and bells and a solid wall of cheers so loud, so overwhelming, that Tom simply stood at the edge of the barge and wondered why he didn't feel a thing.

The long line of limousines and Rolls-Royces paraded back to Las Vegas and the awards ceremony at

Caesar's Palace.

Katie was sharing a sleek stretch Lincoln with Maycee and Molly and Hugh. She'd longed to see Tom and hold him in her arms, but the contestants were kept separate from the others, thanks to some archaic rule of pyrotechnic protocol.

There had been that initial elation over the beauty and power of the performance, but that elation had faded as quickly as the fireworks themselves. It was Tom they were all thinking about.

"When do we get to see Tom and Ed again?" she asked as they approached the lights of Las Vegas.

"They'll be on the dais with the others," Molly said, "but we won't have a chance to talk to them until the entire ceremony is over."

"That's ridiculous."

Molly laughed. "That's standard operating procedure in this industry. The more ridiculous the rules, the better they like it."

So it would seem.

When they entered the ballroom at Caesar's twenty minutes later, the place was swarming with media. Enormous lights, hot and blinding, surrounded the raised stage and hung from the ceiling.

Photographers circled the crowd like hungry tigers. Twice Katie was stopped by eager paparazzi, only to be relegated to the sidelines when they realized she wasn't material for *People* or the *Star*.

She took her seat at the Sagan table. Maycee chain-smoked at one end; Molly bit her nails at the other; Hugh drummed his fingertips on the tabletop. Katie's stomach tied itself into knots Sinbad the Sailor would have envied.

The entire room hummed with nervous tension in five languages while the whirring TV cameras recorded it all for tomorrow's morning news. A rumor made the rounds that David Hartman and Jane Pauley were vying for the first interview with the winner.

There was a decidedly carnival atmosphere, but neither Katie nor anyone else at their table felt like celebrating. For them, winning was not a question of publicity or acclaim. Winning was a way for one man to make peace with himself.

At last the house lights dimmed. The contestants filed in and took their seats on the dais. Tom had changed back into his tux for the ceremony, and he looked to Katie like a Greek god come down to earth to mingle with the mortals.

Love, fierce and protective, made it difficult for her to sit politely in her seat when what she wanted was to be at his side.

The emcee droned on over the incongruous parade music filtering in from somewhere else in the hotel complex.

Katie leaned over toward Molly. "Why do I keep expecting them to play 'Hail to the Chief'?"

"Shh," Molly said, putting her finger to her lips. "Don't give them any ideas."

Katie's remark was passed up and down the length of the table. A few of the old-timers flashed her a thumbs-up sign and she smiled. She felt as if she'd always been a part of them and they, a part of her. If only Tom—

Her thoughts were cut off by a drumroll.

"Third place in the Second Biennial International Fireworks Competition goes to Henri Boudreau and his crew from Lyons, France."

Henri and his defiantly well-coiffed wife went up to the podium and gave an acceptance speech worthy of the Academy Awards.

On stage, Tom and Ed exchanged quick glances. Katie's heart was thumping so wildly that she felt it in her throat and in her temples.

"Second place in the Second Biennial International Fireworks Competition goes to—" the emcee paused coyly and Katie wished she had a spare rocket launcher under the table "—the Ogatsu family, the pride of Japan."

Maycee stifled a small cry and grabbed for her cigarettes. Molly held onto Hugh's arm as if he were the last solid object on earth.

Katie watched the man she loved as he sat there and waited; she felt every ounce of his pain and guilt and tension as if it were her own.

And why not?

Since that day on the train in the mountains of Hakone, he had been part of her heart.

An assistant brought out an enormous silver trophy complete with a winged Zeus cum thunderbolt.

"It's ours," one of the old-timers at the table said. "We nailed that blue."

"I'm worried about the Brits," another one argued. "Their waterfall was the best I've seen since Monte Carlo in 1977."

"Shut up," Molly hissed.

Katie concurred.

The emcee smiled for the TV cameras and caressed the trophy. "It's a beauty, isn't it?" He gestured toward the competitors remaining on the stage. "Only one of those fine pyrotechnicians can win this award." He accepted a white envelope sealed with red wax from a statuesque brunette in a matching red evening gown and held it up for the cameras. "And only I know the answer."

"What is this?" Katie muttered. "The Miss America contest?"

"All of our competitors were truly extraordinary. When you deal with talent like this, there are never any losers. In fact, why don't we give them all a big round of applause right now?"

"I can't take any more," Katie said to Molly. "One more stale joke and I'm going to grab that damned envelope away from him!"

Molly laughed despite her nervousness. "Only if I get to strangle him with his own cummerbund."

The applause died down.

The emcee ripped open the envelope. Katie watched as a piece of red wax dropped to the floor of the dais.

Please, she whispered silently, *let him win.*

"And the winner of the grand prize in the Second Biennial International Fireworks Festival is—" The drumroll thundered toward a crescendo "Sagan Fireworks of Las Vegas!"

The ballroom exploded with excitement, and cool, logical Katie Powers started to cry.

"Go on up there, son!" Ed McTavitt's voice somehow penetrated the fog Tom was in. "Go up there and collect that prize!"

Tom got up and approached the podium. Reporters climbed over the foot of the stage, thrusting microphones forward to catch his first words as if they were gold coins. Photographers raised their Nikons high and clicked wildly, trying to nail that first flush of raw emotion.

It was public recognition of a very private triumph and suddenly he wanted no part of it.

"I—" He stopped and cleared his throat. "I want to thank you all for this honor. It is something—" What in hell was the matter with him? His voice was getting husky with emotions he couldn't control. He coughed and tugged at his bow tie, then leaned toward the microphone again. "Maycee, would you come up here?"

The audience murmured as his mother made her way to the podium. He turned toward Ed and motioned for the man to join them.

"This isn't mine," he said, unable to stop tears from welling up. "This would have belonged to Buck and Paula. Now it belongs to both of you."

Before his mother could say anything or Ed could grab him in another bear hug or the photographers could drop into position for a wonderful group shot, Tom vaulted over the side of the stage and headed for the door.

He had to get the hell out of there before Katie saw him cry.

Katie watched as Tom left the ballroom.

Not this time, she thought.

This time she couldn't run after him. He had walked right by her table and out that door as if he didn't know her.

She certainly didn't know him.

When all the talk of love at first sight and grand gestures and Lady Luck was over, the bare-bones fact of the matter was that he didn't really need her. She had been part of the obsession that had consumed him, but not really a part of his heart.

His secrets, his passions, his sorrows still remained his alone.

Oh, the significance of his coming to Boston when he should have been working toward the contest wasn't lost on her. She couldn't have spent these past two days with his family and friends and not have picked up on the degree of obsessive dedication he'd brought to the endeavor.

That she could understand.

But grand gestures didn't matter a damn if they weren't backed up by a foundation of trust that could withstand life's stormier weather. Sharing sorrow was trickier than sharing joy: it required the painful act of revealing the true heart beneath the valentine. The ultimate leap of faith.

Without it, love didn't stand a chance.

She and Robert had found that out.

And from the looks of it, so had she and Tom.

She glanced at her evening purse that held her ticket back to Boston.

Return postage guaranteed.

Too bad she could no longer see the humor in that.

What in hell was the matter with him?

Tom stood in the hallway outside the ballroom.

For eighteen months he'd worked toward this day. For eighteen months he'd eaten, breathed, dreamed of how it would feel to bring that damned trophy home to the Sagan company, just as Buck and Paula would have wanted.

And now that he had, now that Ed and Maycee shared the trophy, now that the dreams and the memories could be put on the mantelpiece along with it, Tom felt empty.

His long-standing guilt had receded in the face of tri-umph, but the elation was surprisingly short-lived.

Without Katie Powers, none of this was worth a damn.

For eighteen months he'd telescoped his life down, until nothing existed but his need to prove himself. Falling in love with Katie had split his heart wide open, and all the pain and fear and emptiness he'd kept bottled up had rushed in on him all at once.

She had welcomed him into her life and let him see her soul, while he had done his level best to make sure that she never saw his, since he felt certain that the human being behind the golden-boy facade would fall short of her expectations.

And maybe he would.

But there was no way they could build a future to-gether—no matter how great the love, how strong the desire—if he didn't take that chance.

Katie was sitting alone at the Sagan table, toying with her glass of champagne, when the hotel manager approached her.

"Ms. Powers?"

She stood up and nodded.

"Would you come with me?"

"Is something wrong?"

"Nothing to be alarmed about. If you would just follow me, your presence is requested in the parking lot."

"The parking lot?" She must have had more to drink than she thought.

"Yes," he said. "Please follow me."

Katie tried her best, but she could get no further in-formation out of the man. She did notice a twinkle in his dark brown eyes, but that did little to relieve her confusion.

They wound their way through a corridor beneath the private casino reserved for high rollers, then stopped before an enormous exit.

He unlocked it and smiled. "Enjoy."

Enjoy?

Katie stepped outside and stared in amazement, for there in the middle of the parking lot stood Tom Sagan surrounded by enough blazing sparklers to illuminate a small city.

"Stop." His voice echoed in the empty courtyard as he walked toward her. "This time it's my turn."

Her heart thudded wildly as he came closer.

"I love you, Katie Powers." He stopped just inches away from her. "And I'm scared as hell of losing you."

"You won't lose me," she said, "not if you let me love you."

"I've made a hell of a lot of mistakes along the way. Mistakes I'm not proud of."

"So have I." She thought of the marriage that might have worked if she'd only had the guts to confront her fears. "The trick is in not making those mistakes a second time."

He stepped closer and she saw the shadows beneath those beautiful eyes, the hint of the real man behind the golden facade. If possible, it made her love him more.

"It won't always be easy," he said. "Life has a way of not playing fair."

"It's worth the risk." It had taken her twenty-eight years to realize that simple fact. "Are you trying to scare me away, Mr. Sagan?"

"No." He took her left hand, the one on which she wore the onyx-and-gold ring, and pressed it to his lips. "I'm asking you to be my wife."

"I love you," she whispered. "More than you know."

"Does that mean yes?"

"Yes!" She threw her head back and laughed into the summer night. "Yes! Yes! Yes!"

His smile was dazzling as he fingered the tape on the back of the onyx ring. "We'll even find you a ring that fits."

"Just you try it. It would mean a lot to me to wear your father's ring."

All of the pain and love and tenderness he'd tried so hard to hide was visible in his eyes.

"My tough New Englander," he murmured against her lips. "Marry me tonight, Katie. Let's take the biggest risk of all."

"Not tonight," she said, taking his hand. "Tonight I have other plans."

With typical Yankee economy, she told him exactly what she had in mind.

"Logical Katie Powers," he said, laughing. "When you're right, you're right."

The golden sparklers faded into memory as Tom and Katie went up to her room to set off a few fireworks of their own.

Epilogue

August 16, three years later   Las Vegas

"You can do it, Katie." Tom's voice floated somewhere near the ceiling. "I'm here, Katie. You can do it."

"I can't. Something's wrong. I know it—"

Pain, more intense, less focused, cut off her words.

"That's it," the doctor said. "We're almost home free. One good push, Katie."

"I can't."

"Just one," Tom said, supporting her shoulders. "We'll do it. Come on ..."

Katie closed her eyes and summoned up strength from every part of her body and soul to push that child into the world.

"Easy ... easy ... it's coming ... it's coming. ..."

The world went black, then red, then a swirling mass of color and pain, and finally a relief so exquisite that she lost consciousness for a second.

When she opened her eyes, she saw her husband's face and felt the warm weight of the baby at her breast.

"We have a daughter," he said, his tears falling freely down his face. "A perfect daughter."

"We did it," she whispered. "Thank God."

He kissed her cheek. "I love you, Katie."

She smiled. Love didn't come close to expressing all she felt for her husband and her child.

The baby wailed and her parents melted.

"Caroline Powers Sagan," Tom said softly. "Welcome home."

It was the night of fireworks and celebration, when the ancestors visited their earthly homes, then followed the stars back to the heavens.

And that night, the sky over Las Vegas blazed with a thousand shooting stars to celebrate the start of a precious new life.

Katie and Tom Sagan had seen their future, and she was perfect.

Just perfect.

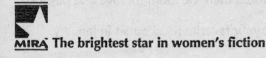

New York Times bestselling author

Heather Graham Pozzessere

With no one else to turn to, she struck a deal with a

Dark Stranger

Tragedy had left Kristin McCahy desperate. The
malicious murder of her father had stripped her of
more than a loved one—she'd lost her independence
and her sense of safety. Stranger Cole Slater, with
a painful past of his own, was the only one who
could help save her ranch and her family. But first,
a bargain would have to be made.

Theirs was a partnership of convenience with the sole
intent of survival. But when the past had been
avenged, would there be room for love and passion?

Available at your favorite retail outlet in January.

When desires run wild,

Confessions

can be deadly

JoAnn Ross

The shocking murder of a senator's beautiful wife has shaken the town of Whiskey River. Town sheriff Trace Callihan gets more than he bargained for when the victim's estranged sister, Mariah Swann, insists on being involved with the investigation.

As the black sheep of the family returning from Hollywood, Mariah has her heart set on more than just solving her sister's death, and Trace, a former big-city cop, has more on his mind than law and order.

What will transpire when dark secrets and suppressed desires are unearthed by this unlikely pair? Because nothing is as it seems in Whiskey River—and everyone is a suspect.

Look for *Confessions* at your favorite retail outlet this January.

If you love the adventurous style of

BARBARA BRETTON

Then order now to receive more romantic tales
by one of MIRA's star authors:

#66004	TOMORROW & ALWAYS	$4.99 U.S.	☐
		$5.50 CAN.	☐
#66044	NO SAFE PLACE	$4.99 U.S.	☐
		$5.50 CAN.	☐
#66090	DESTINY'S CHILD	$4.99 U.S.	☐
		$5.50 CAN.	☐

(limited quantities available)

TOTAL AMOUNT	$
POSTAGE & HANDLING	$
($1.00 for one book, 50¢ for each additional)	
APPLICABLE TAXES*	$_____
TOTAL PAYABLE	$_____

(check or money order—please do not send cash)

To order, send the completed form with your name, address, zip or postal
code, along with a check or money order for the total above, payable to
MIRA Books, to: **In the U.S.:** 3010 Walden Avenue, P.O. Box 9077,
Buffalo, NY 14269-9077; **In Canada:** P.O. Box 636, Fort Erie, Ontario, L2A
5X3.

Name: _____

Address: _____ City: _____

State/Prov.: _____ Zip/Postal Code: _____

*New York residents remit applicable sales taxes.
 Canadian residents remit applicable GST and provincial taxes.   MBBBL4

MIRA